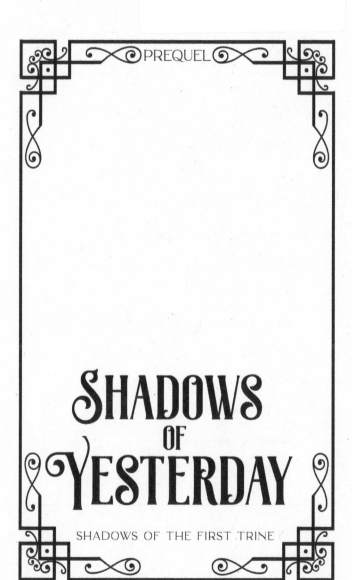

PREQUEL

SHADOWS
OF
YESTERDAY

SHADOWS OF THE FIRST TRINE

Shadows of Yesterday

This is a work of fiction. Names, characters, businesses, places, events,

and incidents are either the product of the author's imagination or are

used !ctitiously. Any resemblance to actual persons, living or dead,

events, or locals is entirely coincidental

Contact info: cleavebourbon@gmail.com

Front Cover Design by Cleave Bourbon

Print Cover Design by Cleave Bourbon

Editor: Courtney Umphress www.courtneyumphress.com

SECOND EDITION : April 2023

10 9 8 7 6 5 4 3 2

SHADOWS OF YESTERDAY

SHADOWS OF THE FIRST TRINE PREQUEL

CLEAVE BOURBON

SHADESILVER PUBLISHING

The Ascene Mts.

Asperden

Falcon Hurst

Borderton

Ardenia

Ardmore

Breckencourt

Distiac River

Rive

Highpond

Dradia River

mond's Arch

Fallwyn

Sythia

The Great Sythian Forest

Foresthome
(Endil)

Arosyth

Trigothia

Arelland

Gothiac River

Crystal Mill

Ostley

Plainview

Lake
Ostley

Adracoria

Kyleia

van

Adrontear

Kragodor

Ishrak

Ðraegodor

Mountains of Madness

Mt. Urieus.

Tyre

The Plain of Storms

Ishva

Tyr Raganough

The Jagged Mountains

Silverton

Symboria

Brookhaven

Watch Hill

Seabrey

The Southern Pass

Basillain

The Tower of Morgoran

Soldier's Bluff

The Southern Road

The Black

The Twin Keeps

Cedar Falls

Roseshade

Signal Hill

Vetell Fex

Valwall

River

Symbor

Old Symbor

The Sacred Land

Arill.

Arillia

CONTENTS

SHADOWS OF THE FIRST TRINE PREQUEL...

They were hardly a threat before.

Sure, the shifters could look like allies, but they weren't good at imitating personalities or the little quirks that make each person unique, and they had a distinctive odor that always gave them away . . . but change is inevitable, and over time, they must have learned how to model the behavior of their chosen identity accurately.

It's even rumored they managed to extinguish the telling smell!

Now, they allegedly walk among unsuspecting folk, virtually undetectable, but the sorceress Lady Shey must set aside her worries about shapeshifting monster to focus on her quest of saving the kingdoms' only hope back into the light—a group of descendants, according to the seers, living a simple life tucked away peacefully in the mountains. The only problem is she might be unwittingly leading the monsters straight to them.

PROLOGUE

The light from the fire pit danced on the walls like little yellow and red sylphs delighting in the ominous workings of the wielder at the center of the room. Dirty, soot-stained green robes clung haphazardly to an emaciated frame of a man at task. Feverishly, he drew in as much essence from his surroundings as possible and concentrated his mental faculties on a single oblong object sitting on the wooden table before him. Scattered on the floor all around the table lay the remains of brightly-colored egg shells, dragon eggshells, to be exact. As he concentrated his power on the egg, the walls of the room buckled outward, and the ceiling groaned from the strain. Sweat began to pour from the wielder's forehead as he concentrated, and just before it seemed the walls would crack open and the ceiling would burst out, he collapsed onto the dirty floor. In delirium, he dreamed about a silver statue of a great dragon with ruby eyes clawing at him. A small green statuette of an elf maiden glowed in his hands, and a young girl of about fifteen seasons with sapphire blue eyes laughed at him.

When he awoke, it was daytime. The only window in the room let in the sunlight. He gathered his strength and stood before the table, searching for the egg. Thankfully it was still intact on the table. All his previous attempts had failed, destroying the egg, but this time he had succeeded. He carefully removed the egg from the table and placed it on a specially-lined stone bowl near the fire pit. The wielder in green robes went about stoking the fire until it roared back into a steady flame. Somewhere in the back of his mind he heard the door open behind him but did not turn to see who entered the room.

"Master?"

The man started at the sound of a human voice. "What, who is it?"

"Master, it is I. It is Naneden."

"Ah yes, Naneden. Come here and gaze upon my work. I have done it. I have moved beyond the creation of Dramyds from dragonkind. I have used the power of the gods and created our greatest ally."

Naneden looked over his master's shoulder at the egg. "Master, what have you created inside this egg?"

"My dear apprentice, what I have created will strike fear in the hearts of men and elf-kind alike, for it will have the ability to blend among them undetected. I have taken an egg of the Drasmyd brood and the essence of the Duil brood and combined their magic into a single egg. When it hatches, this new Drasmyd Duil will not only be able to create Dramyd at a far more prolific rate; it will be able to use the magic of the Duil dragons to take the shape of whatever creature it desires."

A wicked grin formed on Naneden's thin lips, "You are talking about the creation of your army of Dramyds. You have done it, Master; you can now produce the great army of Toborne."

"Did you doubt me?"

"No, Master, I have never doubted you."

"We will need a greater number of dragon eggs from the two broods. Can you manage it?"

"Stealing the eggs is dangerous, my master, but with the help of the Dramyds you have already created, I should be able to take what we need. Of course, the number of egg-producing dragons dwindles as we manipulate them."

Toborne's brow furled in concentration. "Yes, ideally we should capture a pair of each for our purposes."

"Master, even if we could do such a thing, dragons of these two broods do not lay clutches of eggs often. Might we learn how to employ the life-birth broods? An army of Drasmyd Duil would surely destroy the Dramyd and the Duil populations."

"The Dramyds will comprise the army. These Drasmyd Duil will have a different purpose."

"We must also take into consideration that the live-birth dragon broods will naturally try to stop us from taking their young and from taking more of their relatives' dragon eggs."

"They will try. Of course, they will send their precious dragon knights out before they will come for us themselves. It is their folly that they put so much faith into their knights. It will buy us time to amass an army large enough to defeat even them."

Naneden thought for a long moment. "Master, if we could some-how control the population of egg-laying broods, we could hatch them to fight against those who would seek to stop us. The drakes could be a powerful ally."

"Naneden, you are wise beyond your many seasons. I was right to apprentice you." Toborne gazed lovingly at his egg by the fire. "There is a way to take control over them. I have tried to do it before, but I failed."

"How, Master?"

"It requires taking control over the Silver Drake. With the power the gods have bestowed upon her, we could ensure our victory in the war to come. It will not be easy. The Silver Drake is a force to be reckoned with, and she is heavily guarded."

Naneden's eyes twinkled with delight. "Master, if you will permit me, I will find a way."

CHAPTER 1

THE REAPER IN THE DARK

"Hurry, we don't have much time. There are at least five Enforcers only a few hours' ride from here. We have to get your daughter, Oria, into The Sacred Land," Lady Shey pleaded.

Del was a big man, muscular and fit. He scratched his brown beard on his kind and pleasant face. "My lady, I still do not understand. I am a strong man. I can protect her here at the farm."

Lady Shey was exasperated. "No, Del, you can't. We've been through this. Oria has a gift that needs to be cultivated. The Enforcers have no use for her. They will kill her! There is nothing you can do."

"Tell me the story one more time."

Lady Shey sat back in her chair by the fire in Del's farmhouse. "You want a history lesson . . . now?"

"How will getting her to The Sacred Land help her? How is that barren land, where there is barely any protection, better than my farm?"

"All right, one more time and then we can go?"

"If you can convince me, aye, we will go."

Out of a sense of urgency, Lady Shey tried to think of a way she could tell the story of The Sacred Land quickly and still convince Del it was time to flee. "In the seasons after the War of the Oracle, the people of Symboria and the other neighboring kingdoms decided to memorialize the huge tract of land devastated by the use of magic and the armaments of war into a vast wasteland by declaring the land sacred."

Del lit his pipe, which made Lady Shey even more furious and leaned back in his chair. "I know of the war and why The Sacred Land was declared sacred."

"I have to start at the beginning, or I will forget parts of the story. Just sit still and smoke your pipe!" She took a deep breath. "Several memorials were dedicated across The Sacred Land to the many men and women who fought and died in the war. At the northern edge of The Sacred Land, twin keeps were constructed. The first keep was named Calanbrough and the second was named Brightonhold. Calanbrough was set up as the home of the Defenders of The Sacred Land, a group of men tasked with patrolling The Sacred Land and keeping it safe from looters and riffraff. Brightonhold Keep was designated the home of the Enforcers, a select group of men chosen to enforce the newly created law against the use of all magic, which several kingdoms adopted. The problem is that many if not all the Enforcers are magic users themselves; that way they can detect users of magic and arrest them more easily." She tried to drive the point home by staring Del in the eyes. "The fact that the Enforcers were policing and executing their own kind was considered an abominable act by the veteran wielders of the War of the Oracle.

"So they track down and kill their own? That is despicable," Del said.

"There's more. People born with the ability to wield magic were either made to join the Enforcers or die. That is why we need to get Oria to The Sacred Land. They usually do not recruit women for their ranks."

"I would not let her join their ranks if they did! But you have not answered my question. Why take her to the barren waste of The Sacred Land?"

"Wielding works, for the most part, by drawing in essence from all things surrounding the wielder. Everything has essence, but living things have the most. If you draw essence from a thing, it will regenerate its essence easily, but if a wielder or group of wielders keep drawing and drawing the same source of essence, they will deplete it completely. Depending on the source, it will kill it or make it dormant for a long time. The War of the Oracle, which created The Sacred Land, made the wasteland. There is no more essence there to draw upon. The Enforcers would not be able to locate her, and the Defenders do not like the Enforcers." Lady Shey could finally see the comprehension in his eyes.

"Ah, all right, I see."

"Good. Let's get Oria and get out of here. We can get ahead of the Enforcers and be in The Sacred Land before morning."

Del put away his pipe. "She sleeps. She was so tired. Can't we wait for a time, just to get her strength back?"

Out of frustration, Lady Shey put her head in her hands, her long, dark hair falling in front of her face. She threw her hair back and smoothed it with her hand, letting it fall down her shoulders. "Del, how can I convince you of the urgency of your situation?"

"You are a wielder, you say. You are also obviously a woman. How is it that you are here and not killed by these Enforcers?"

"I am a master wielder. At different times, throughout my training, I was apprenticed to every member of the First Trine. I am also an advisor to the court of Symboria. I am exempt from the law."

"You were apprenticed once to Ianthill, Morgoran, and Toborne?"

"Aye, I was apprenticed to Toborne when I was about fourteen seasons and then to Morgoran until his curse by the Silver Drake. Finally, Ianthill continued my training to master wielder."

The conversation was interrupted by the sound of horse hooves pounding up to the house. Del sat up, alert. Lady Shey looked at him with concern that changed to dread. She knew who rode those horses. A moment later, there was a pounding at the door. Del got up to answer it at Shey's nod.

When the door opened, a man in a dark grey cloak pushed his way in. "I am Captain Vose of the Enforcers. We have a report that a young woman here is afflicted."

Lady Shey stood up. "Aye, I am a wielder, not afflicted as you so call it."

He took a step closer to her. "You admit it!"

"I am Lady Shey Namear, the advisor of Highlord Rastafin Stowe of the city of Lux Enor." She leaned in for effect. "You say you are Captain Vose? How dare you burst in here like that!"

The captain was taken aback for a split second but recovered. "The one we seek is younger than you, my lady. Your station will not have any bearing on this matter."

Del took the opportunity to throw a punch at the captain, knocking him to the floor. He pounced on the Enforcer, hitting him repeatedly. The other Enforcers came in and eventually held him back.

Del looked at Lady Shey with hurt in his eyes. "You will not use your gifts to defend us?"

"I told you of the danger you were facing, Del. You kept us here for far too long."

Captain Vose cracked a wicked smile. "The girl is ours, then. Find her, men."

Shey stepped forward. "Not so fast, Captain. Her father might be a fool, but I will still defend the girl. You see, I take care of our own, unlike you who would see your own mother burn if she was, how did you put it, afflicted!"

Captain Vose laughed, and his men followed suit. "You will defend these people against all of us? Five wielders against one wielder and an unarmed man!"

Lady Shey reached beneath her robes and produced two curved silver daggers. "Aye, that's right."

Captain Vose drew his sword. Lady Shey knew it was imbued against magic; all the Enforcer weapons were to prevent them from being vulnerable. Shey began to draw essence, and she could see by the surprise on Vose's face that he had not expected her to do that right in front of him.

"Kill him!" Vose commanded.

Shey released the essence into her daggers as she threw them at the two Enforcers holding Del. The blades made several lightning quick attacks, piecing key points on both men. They fell clutching their necks where blood poured out of deadly wounds. The daggers returned to her hands, and she threw them again at the other two Enforcers who were trying to come through the door. She felt them trying to draw essence, but their ability to use magic was far beneath what it took to stop Shey's dagger attacks. They tried to fend them off with swords, but the quick daggers were relentless. Next, they went to Vose's sword arm, causing him to drop it. Del managed to clutch the startled captain's throat. Shey's daggers returned to her, clean and shiny. She put them away underneath her robes.

"Perhaps if you trained your magical abilities more, you could compete with a master wielder, Captain. Your magical abilities are almost non-existent, and I am no mere novice."

He tried to speak, and Shey nodded to Del to let him. "You lose, wielder. We already knew of your presence. Captain Row Praf is on his way here with ten men."

Lady Shey suddenly appeared worried. She nodded to Del, who dragged the captain out into the yard. He returned a few moments later. "I—"

Shey held up her hand to stop him. "I don't want to know what you did with him. I abhor killing indiscriminately like this." She looked him in the eye, and he took a step back. "You believe me now? The blood of these men is on your hands. We could have avoided this bloodshed. Now, go get Oria and get her ready to travel. I have heard of Captain Praf. He was a wielder during the War of the Oracle. He will not be so easy for me to defeat, especially if ten men accompany him." She wondered if she sounded too harsh, but she knew she couldn't afford to wait any longer. She looked down at the four men on the floor and turned away. Such a waste, five wielders for the life of one.

Del disappeared into the back of the farmhouse to get his daughter.

Del's farm was located just west of the capital city of Symbor in the kingdom of Symboria. All Shey had to do was lead them directly west to get to the Sacred Land. She was afraid that Captain Praf might be coming from the northwest and would intercept them, so she stayed to the coast as much as possible.

Lady Shey rode her horse next to Del, and Oria rode just behind her father. After a long silence, Del spoke. "I want to apologize, my lady. I was skeptical of your story until the Enforcers actually showed up. I should have believed you."

"Aye, you should have. I have other duties to perform besides running all over the countryside trying to rescue novice wielders." She intentionally softened her expression. She could tell by his face that Del was genuinely sorry. "What is done is done. Don't be too hard on yourself. Wielders that hunt wielders are the lowest of people, in my opinion. I am not in the habit of killing them, but I know from experience that they have no qualms about killing other wielders." She hesitated because she didn't want to frighten Oria. She decided to say it, anyway, just phrased gentler. "They would have done terrible things to Oria."

"I had heard of Enforcers. I thought they were around to protect us," Del said.

"No matter how barbaric some people thought the magic law was, life continued on after the War of the Oracle in relative peace, so no one questioned the Enforcers' authority. Their leaders have spent a lot of time and effort to cover up some of their atrocities and rebuild their reputation.

"They only go after potential wielders, then?"

"Not always. There is a select few who display the ability to use mental abilities called the wild magic. They are largely exiled rather than killed, because of their tendency to slay several Enforcers at their moment of execution. Only the weak afflicted with wild magic are executed now."

"You do not believe Enforcers are here for the greater good?"

"You are remarkably uninformed about the Enforcers to be a child of Symboria. Most Symborian children are taught to hate wielders and magic. In fact, they have been known to turn over their own family to Enforcers when they discovered the ability." She stopped her horse and studied Del for a moment.

Del let his horse come to a natural stop. "It's different when the accused is your own. I would never turn over my own flesh and blood."

Shey considered Oria, who had not said a word the whole trip. The girl looked at her and then at Del and then back to her. Lady Shey pulled out her dagger. She moved between Del and Oria. "Who are you? How did you come across this girl?" Shey could see several horsemen riding from the northwest and a rider coming from behind. "What have you done?"

Del held his hand up, and the girl, Oria, began to choke. She fell off her horse. Shey got off her horse and went to her defense.

"I won't kill her . . . yet. I just want to make sure you don't run. You can't resist, can you? You could ride off right now and be free, but you will stay beside this insignificant novice wielder wench. Pathetic!"

"I should have known! No decent person in Symboria would just sit around and wait for Enforcers to come and take their daughter away. You barely lifted a finger to help when they did come."

"You just said that some would turn over their own."

"They aren't who I consider to be decent people. Who would lead their own children off to slaughter?"

"So you said it to test me, then."

"I must admit that concerned people are usually shocked when I tell them such a horrible thing, but not you. You said the right words, but you showed no emotion, a dead giveaway."

"I will have to remember that the next time I entrap a lawbreaker."

The rider from behind came to a stop. It was Captain Vose, alive and well. "Good work, Lieutenant. This wielder has to answer for four Enforcer deaths now on top of charges of harboring wielders."

Lady Shey cracked a smile. "You really don't know who I am, do you?"

"Lady, you could be the queen of Symboria for all I care."

Del pointed to the riders in the northeast. "Is that Captain Row Praf and his men?"

"Your guess is as good as mine. I did, however, send for reinforcements."

"I thought you said Captain Praf and ten men were on their way."

"I was bluffing."

A few moments later, the men arrived. There were four men led by a captain, all in dark grey cloaks.

"What do we have here?" the captain asked.

Captain Vose grabbed Shey's arm. "Enforcer killer, and worse, a wielder. She brings this girl with her to teach her the dark crafts." He reached into her cloak, found her daggers, and disarmed her.

"You're a fool, Vose. This is Lady Shey of Lux Enor. She has the eyes and ears of the highlord. She can have your head on a whim," the captain said.

"Not if we take hers first. If we leave her bones out in The Sacred Land, no one would ever know."

"Put her back on her horse with the girl. The Sacred Land isn't far."

"Aye, sir." He poked Shey. "You heard him—mount up." He grabbed the girl who began to whimper until Shey calmed her with a caress of the girl's face and a shake of her head when the girl looked up at her.

The Enforcers led Lady Shey and the girl across the border into The Sacred Land and kept riding for a few more hours. Shey knew they were not far from the Defender outpost where she was planning on taking the girl anyway by the time they stopped.

The captain ordered her down from her horse. "Rope?" he asked one of his men.

When he had the rope in hand, he began to tie up Lady Shey. He slipped a small stone into the palm of her hand instead of tying the rope. He tapped her on the forearm to let her know he was ready. She pushed him back into her horse, flung open her cloak, and called her daggers to her. They ripped their way from Vose and returned to their sheaths on Shey's waist. She gave Vose a wicked smile, grabbed ahold of the girl, and used the dragon stone the captain had given her. She appeared at the Defender outpost a moment later.

The girl was stunned. "What happened?"

"That captain was really my friend, Lyrrath. He had a personal Lora Daine, a dragon stone."

Shey could see Oria didn't know what a Lora Daine was. "It's a small stone that dragon knights use to transport themselves over short distances. It's dragon magic, the only magic that will work in The Sacred Land. Usually, one this size can only send one person, but you and I are small enough it was able to send us both. Don't worry about it. Just be glad I had my friend check on us."

She took the girl and walked into the wooden outpost building. Once inside, she helped herself to some bittering tea, which was boiling on the small metal stove. A woman in blue robes sat at the desk, writing on parchment.

"I see Lyrrath found you," the woman said.

"What was that?" Shey said, still pouring the dark, fragrant liquid into a small tin cup.

"The Lora Daine. You used the stone."

"Aye." She handed the stone over to the woman. "You will see Lyrrath gets it back, won't you?"

"Certainly." She stopped writing and motioned for Oria to come to her.

"Go on. Oria, this is Enowene. She will instruct you."

The girl went to Enowene. "You will never have to worry about anything as long as you are in my care."

Lady Shey bent down to the girl. "You will be okay now if I leave you with Enowene?"

The girl nodded and hugged Shey. "That man. He wouldn't let me talk. He did something to me. Will I be able to do that too?"

"That and more if you study hard and listen to Enowene."

"I will. No one will do anything like that to me ever again!"

Shey blew on her bittering tea. "Before I travel back to Lux Enor, you want me to go to the ruins of the Temple of the Oracle?"

"Aye, something is stirring up The Sacred Land. The Defenders that occupy this outpost are out patrolling an area where the dead are said to walk this very moment again."

"Is there any truth to it?"

"I came from my old tower in Old Symbor and traveled here across the middle of The Sacred Land and saw nothing out of the ordinary." She reached into her knapsack and produced a blue checkered cloth and handed it to Oria. "Are you hungry, dear?"

The girl nodded and took the cloth. Inside was bread, cheese, and dried, seasoned beef.

Shey took another drink from her cup. "Why do you want me to go to the ruins?"

"It's Morgoran. I know his predictions mostly do not come true, but he has been spouting something about the Oracle of late. He says

The Sacred Land is regaining its essence and with it, the Oracle will return. Ianthill believes you should go there and look it over."

"I noticed I could now draw in small amounts of essence here in the outer edges of the Sacred Land, so that much of his prediction is true at least. Why didn't Ianthill come and see for himself?"

"Ha! Do you really think that one of the great First Trine would do something so trivial? Your master, my brother, has far more important things to do than chase after Morgoran's visions."

Shey put the empty tin cup back where she found it. "All right, the ruins of the temple it is. Is there a horse for me in the stables?"

"Aye, there is."

"Enowene, those men we escaped from, they are not far from here. The man, Del, he can sense her. Lyrrath might lead them away, but it's possible they will come here."

"The Defenders of The Sacred Land will have something to say about that. They are due back at any moment, and if they find Enforcers anywhere near here, there will be blood. Don't worry."

Lady Shey kissed Oria on the top of her head. "I will see you soon, child. You listen to Enowene. She trained me, too, once upon a time."

"I will," Oria said between bites.

Shey gathered her cloak about her and left for the stables.

CHAPTER 2

THE SACRED LAND

S hey bent down to one knee and scooped up a handful of earth. She let the dirt filter between her fingers. *The Sacred Land doesn't feel different than any other dirt*, she thought. The low, heavy clouds made the Sacred Land appear sinister as far as she could see, which was fitting given the land's history. Still, her horse had been acting spooked since the moment they left the outpost. Leading her steed by the reins, she walked along the barren wasteland. No trees grew anymore in The Sacred Land, and the ones that had been there before were like twisted, dead fingers reaching desperately for the grey sky. The further she entered the Sacred Land, the more the dirt beneath her feet felt dead and colorless. Still, she soldiered on.

About midday, she stopped to have a bite to eat. She had to carry food for her horse since there was no grass for it to graze on. She sat down on a dead log and opened up the food pack she had brought.

The day's lunch consisted of dried beef and a hefty portion of cheese. The sheer desolation of The Sacred Land took its toll on any weary traveler. There were no animals, no plant life, no sign of people as far as the eye could see. It was also difficult to mark distance and time once one traveled far enough into the interior. Lady Shey didn't want to spend any more time being idle than she had to, even to eat.

Once again on horseback, Lady Shey decided to make better time to her destination. It was midafternoon by the sun's position when she caught sight of her journey's end. She reached the site and dismounted. The ground and surrounding area didn't appear any different from the greyish, lifeless earth she'd been passing on all day. A lone marker signified the difference; this was the spot of a great sacrifice. Lady Shey went to her saddlebags and removed a single red rose and placed it at the foot of the marker.

"I miss your face," she said.

"I'm sure she misses yours too," a male voice from somewhere behind her said.

Even though Lady Shey had been expecting Gondrial, she was still startled enough by his sudden low male voice to bound into the defensive. "Gondrial. You know better than to sneak up on people." She immediately relaxed once she confirmed it was him.

"I didn't realize I was sneaking." He held his arms out and gestured back and forth. "There isn't a person around for miles. You can practically see the ocean from here it's so flat. Who else would even venture out here in this barren landscape?"

"I was preoccupied, and this barren land isn't so barren anymore. It's beginning to regenerate its essence. Can you sense it?"

"I hadn't tried, to be completely honest. I just assumed it was just as devoid of magic as ever."

"It's just a hint. I managed to use my magic today at the fringes." Her expression changed with her thoughts, "You made good time."

"I have to admit; I did travel here as fast as I could. Traveling across The Sacred Land alone requires one to be of particularly strong will." He found a fallen log nearby and kicked it into a suitable position to sit on or lean against as a backrest. "I had no idea there might have been underlying essence, or I might have taken a bit more time."

"I know you detest the Sacred Land."

"It's the lack of magic; it makes me uncomfortable." He twisted and squinched his face. Shey knew he was probably trying to summon essence. "Even with the minuscule amount, I can detect now." He said.

"It makes me uncomfortable as well. That's why I asked Enowene to send you to meet me here," Shey said.

"Oh, were you planning on traveling with me to Brookhaven, then?"

"Brookhaven? I thought you were going to return with me to Lux Enor."

"You know how I feel about Lux Enor. Too many aristocrats and snobs."

"You mean too many angry husbands?"

Gondrial folded his arms. "I think you might be jumping to conclusions."

"Aye, the right conclusions!" Shey said.

"I've hardly angered any husbands in at least a few months."

"A few months? I would bet all the gold in my pocket; it was more like a few days."

"I would agree with you, but then we'd both be wrong!" Gondrial unfolded his arms and produced his smoking pipe and a medium sized silver flask.

"Well, that's what I believe, knowing you as well as I do."

"Everybody has to believe something. In fact, I believe I'll have a drink and a smoke."

"Of course, you will, at any opportunity."

Gondrial stuffed his pipe with tabac and lit it afterward, puffing clouds of white smoke as he did. He leaned back against the dead log and took a long pull from the flask in his other hand. "The light is fading. It might be a good idea to unpack our camping gear, assuming you want to set up camp here."

"I suppose this is as good a spot as any," Shey said. She joined him at the fallen log. Gondrial handed her the flask. She took a drink from it and almost choked.

"Cliché," he said.

"What?"

"Taking a drink and choking on it. How cliché of you."

"Don't call me cliché! Shey grinned, "What is that swill?"

"Corn mash whiskey."

Shey's grin turned thoughtful, "You didn't have to come, you know."

Gondrial puffed his pipe and let out a wispy cloud of smoke. "Please, sit back and relax." He took another drink when Shey handed the flask back to him. "You know I would never turn you down even if you did ask me to come into the middle of this godforsaken, soul-sucking battlefield. When was the last time you traveled here, anyway?"

"It's been a while. I didn't really want to come, but Ianthill wanted me to. Morgoran has been having visions. I also met a Defender patrol earlier today who thought it was a good idea."

"What did they tell you?"

"They said there had been strange sightings at night, reports of people wandering around, unexplained lights as if someone is carrying a torch around. There have even been reports of unknown flying creatures. They thought now, this moment in time would be a good time for me to investigate."

He coughed out another puff of smoke. "Weird things are roaming around out here, and you're just telling me this now!"

"Cliché!"

"Yes, coughing on my smoke. I see what you did there, very good."

"Oh, relax, Gondrial," Shey said nonchalantly. "I'll protect you if something strange should appear. You needn't worry. Oh, and I also caught that 'unload our camping gear' comment."

"And?"

"And I think you should slow down on that swill you're drinking; you don't want to unpack our gear while drunk. You might stumble and break your fool neck!"

Gondrial rolled his eyes. "I should be so lucky." He put his pipe back into his mouth and took a deep pull, idly gazing into the distance. Suddenly, he lowered his pipe and squinted, then he froze.

Shey could see in Gondrial's far-off gaze that he had spotted something. She peered in the same direction. "What is it? What do you see?"

"Something on the horizon. Do you see it?"

"I don't know what I'm supposed to see. What is it?"

"If I knew what it was, I would tell you." He stood up and put his hand to his forehead to block the light from his eyes. He was looking almost directly into the setting sun. "There's something silhouetted against the sun, but I can't make it out. The sun's too bright."

Shey squinted. "I think I see it, but it's too big to be a man silhouetted at this distance. Could it be a horse or a rider on a horse?"

"It's too far away." He looked away from the sun. "It's probably nothing. It can be as little as blowing dust accentuated against the sun."

"I wonder if this is the sort of thing that has been reported to us by the Defenders?"

Gondrial went to his horse and started to inspect his saddlebags, pulling out items to set up camp. "At any rate, there's nothing we can do about it way out here." He unloaded his sword and gave it a swing. "We'll just have to be vigilant and keep watch."

She found Gondrial swinging a sword comical. "Do you even know how to use that?"

"I had some training when I was younger. I still remember." He jabbed the point of the sword into the ground beside the fallen log. "The question is do you have any way of defending yourself without being able to draw essence?"

Lady Shey brushed aside her cloak and produced her two wicked silver-plated daggers. She began twirling both daggers with masterful skill, finally lodging them in the ground at Gondrial's feet. "Will these do?"

"I forgot about those. All right, I'll take first watch," Gondrial said. "I usually stay up late, anyway. You should try to get some sleep."

Lady Shey looked at Gondrial as if he had lost his mind. "Whatever we saw on the horizon, it's worrisome enough for me to stay awake for a few hours. If it doesn't bother you, why don't you go to sleep and I'll take the first watch."

"Suit yourself. It's a bit early for me with the sun just setting, but far be it from me not to try. I'm sure it was nothing out there, but dust blowing in the wind, now that I think about it." He produced a second flask out from under his leather vest. "On second thought, I will hit the sack just as soon as it gets dark." He took a drink from the flask.

"How quickly your worry has faded. Don't you think you should lay off the drinking tonight?"

"On the contrary, I should drink. It might help sleep come."

"It will probably help stupidity come too." She muttered.

"What did you say?"

"Nothing important. You're really not concerned?"

"I don't worry about matters that are out of my control. We are both in the middle of The Sacred Land, so we can't draw enough essence to use magic effectively, we have meager fighting skills, and night is falling. Whatever will happen will happen, and there's nothing we can do about it now. So, a little drink to take the edge off is warranted in this situation." He held the flask up in the air to accentuate his last statement. "I just remembered the last time I was in this wasteland, all sorts of dirt blowing around. It was unpleasant, and I couldn't wait to leave."

"So, you're scared."

"Terrified!" He took a long drink.

After nightfall, it didn't take long for Gondrial to fall asleep and begin snoring. Shey suspected the alcohol; maybe it wasn't such a bad idea. Restless, she walked the perimeter of the camp, occasionally gazing at the stars, which were bright and brilliant. Alerted to the faint noise of what sounded like an animal's whimper, she stopped and listened. She felt a slight tremor beneath her feet, and she looked back at Gondrial, who was still fast asleep. Without any effort, she abruptly felt essence flow into her body. She didn't draw any essence; it just entered her on its own. The essence felt different somehow, more powerful, easier to control. The tips of her fingers and the tips of her toes tingled. Before her eyes, near the ground marker, two white, partially transparent apparitions appeared. They floated toward her, but she was not afraid.

"How can this be?" Shey asked. "It must be what Ianthill spoke about.

The apparition floated nearer, "Do not fear. I have returned to these lands to seek you out, Sheyna of the Vale of Morgoran."

"You have me at a disadvantage," Shey said.

"I am Ashonda of Symboria. Do you not know me?"

"Ashonda died here in the War of the Oracle."

"Aye, I did. The veil between this world and the next grows thin here."

"Why, what has changed?"

"The power of the land is returning. Those who perished here are part of that power. Our bodies lie buried beneath this magic torn soil. We are the essence of the land returning at least in part."

"I see. This is what Morgoran sees in his tortured second sight!"

"I cannot speak of such things, for I know nothing about them. Such speculations are for another time; this isn't a social visit," Ashonda asserted. "We have business." She pointed her finger at Gondrial. "Awaken!"

Gondrial sprang to life as if he were stung by a scorpion. "Who's that, who's there?"

"I'm called Ashonda."

Still visibly shaken, Gondrial joined Lady Shey. "Is this real, or am I dreaming?"

"If you're dreaming, we're sharing it," Lady Shey said. He promptly pinched her arm.

"Ouch, why are you pinching me?

"To see if I'm dreaming,"

"You're supposed to pinch yourself."

"I like this way better." He pinched her again.

"Ouch stop it! You imbecile!"

Gondrial nonchalantly reached over to Lady Shey's arm once more and gave her another pinch. She yanked her arm away. "It's real," she said.

"So, you are a ghost or what?" Gondrial asked.

"She is an essence ghost." Shey told him, "the barrier between her world and this world is thin."

"It fortunate you have come here?" Ashonda said, her ethereal countenance twisted in a disapproving frown. "Although Ianthill's choice of apprentices seems to have wavered in the years."

Shey caught the insult and knew it was a jab at Gondrial, but she decided to press on before he realized it and delayed the encounter further, "There have been reports of strange happenings here. Activity in The Sacred Land. Morgoran Cleareyes, the man cursed to only see into the future, sent me here to investigate."

"Indeed, there have," Ashonda said. "It is as you and I have suggested; the Sacred Land is awakening; essence and life are returning. Over the next few years, the Sacred Land will return to the way it was before the War of the Oracle; however, it's essence will be tenfold and therefore much more powerful, as a burned grassy field returns all the greener so shall the essence return to this battlefield."

Gondrial scratched his head. "So, what is it you want?"

"You mustn't let the Oracle awaken with The Sacred Land." Ashonda gestured outward toward the open wasteland, "I am here," Ashonda continued "because my bloodline is connected to this land and the task at hand. You must seek out my bloodline, Shey. If the Oracle should arise, only my bloodline will be able to banish him again since it was I who banished him before. I am linked to him now." She paused for a long moment as Shey felt a surge of essence travel through her. The apparition floated closer, "The bloodline of Ardenia also holds sway. The bloodline of Marella Arden is as important as my heritage. During the War of the Oracle, my family had a farm my father named Brookhaven. It is my understanding my family's farm has now grown into a village called by the same name. My line still lives there along with a family from Ardenia, the Adair family."

"I know that place," Gondrial said. "It's nestled up in the foothills of the Jagged Mountains." He turned to Shey, "Magic is outlawed there."

Lady Shey nodded.

Ashonda continued, "I am here because the power of The Sacred Land is regenerating and those who gave their lives here are tied closely to it. Morgoran's visions are but one warning of what is to come. What we started all those many years ago is not yet finished. It falls on you and our descendants to secure the future."

"What does that mean?" Shey asked. "Will there be a second War of the Oracle?"

Ashonda began to fade. "That is up to you and the strength we left behind in our lineage; therefore, it is up to my generation's legacy now. You must not let it come to pass. The only certainty I can give you is that the Oracle will return with the renewal of The Sacred Land and the key to controlling the power The Sacred Land brings is in Brookhaven." With those words, the apparition of Ashonda faded completely away.

Gondrial kicked absently at the ground. "That's just great. Is this an advantage, knowing about Brookhaven?"

"What do you mean?"

"I mean it's only a matter of time before those seeking to take control of the power of The Sacred Land will find out about it as well. We need to get to Brookhaven."

"Actually, I think running directly off to Brookhaven would be a mistake. I think we should regroup and travel there independently. If either of us is being followed, it will give us time to throw them off our trail. You remember the detection spell I taught you?"

"Of course."

"Good, we should go there in a roundabout way."

"Is it that serious? What are you not telling me?"

"Well, this isn't the first time Morgoran has seen something in his visions about Brookhaven. Ianthill already has Sanmir there keeping an eye on things. He will alert us if there is any immediate danger." She placed her forefinger to her lips, "In fact, perhaps you should meander toward Brookhaven as discussed and tell Sanmir what we have learned. Instead of following you, I will go back to Lux Enor and get my affairs in order with the highlord. If you discover anything out of the ordinary, send word, and I will make some excuse to travel in that direction."

Gondrial agreed. He pulled his sword from the ground. "Get some sleep. I will keep watch for a couple of hours."

Lady Shey set up her bedroll, but no matter how she tried, sleep would not come. She had too much on her mind. Then, just as sleep began to take her, she felt the familiar surge of essence. It jolted her awake in time to see another apparition appear. At first, the white-bearded man looked serene and agreeable, but the closer he came, the more horrifying his appearance became. Shey rubbed the sleep from her eyes and looked again. The apparition came close, and Shey reared back, reaching to wake Gondrial.

"Gondrial! Gondrial, wake up!" He did not stir.

"Lady Shey of the Vale of Morgoran!" The apparition said, his face the visage of a white-bearded skull now.

Shey turned back to Gondrial; he stirred but still did not wake.

"Lady Shey of the Vale of Morgoran!" The bearded skull repeated.

"I am," Shey said. "Who are you?"

"They are coming. They are coming for you!"

"Who? Who is coming for me."

"The abominations, they seek you out. You must forget all you have learned here. You were sent here to be deceived." He began to fade out physically.

"No, wait! Don't go; I don't understand!" The surge of essence returned for a brief moment and then the spirit was gone.

"Hmm, well that was unexpected."

Shey was startled by the sudden sound of a voice flanking her. She glanced back at Gondrial, but he just turned and let out a stifled snore. It wasn't him. She backed up and frantically searched for the source of the voice.

"Over here. I didn't startle you, did I? Surely not after that thing."

"Kyrie? Is that you?"

"Aye, a version of me." An elf about the size of a six-year-old human boy stepped out of the shadows and sat on the fallen log where Gondrial had sat earlier. He wore a green and white tunic with fancy embroidery and a green hat with a feather. He held out a length of stick and pointed it at the fire, which sprang back to life when he touched the end of the wood to the embers. "Your fire is almost out. There that's better."

"What do you mean a version of you? What is that you're wearing?"

He stood and bowed, "Kyrie Keeperstone at your service." He sat back down on the fallen log. "These are my fancy clothes. I always wear them when in the Sacred Land. They make me feel better. Have you looked around? This place is very gloomy, very gloomy indeed."

"Answer me."

"I mean that I am not really here, not really. I have projected myself here, but I am trapped in a place not too far away."

"Where, I will come to rescue you."

"Oh, no, I'm trapped but not hurt or anything, and I can move freely like I am now. No, you have your mission. I'm fine the way I am. Besides, I am waiting for someone special to come along soon, not that you aren't special, mind you, but this person will need me."

"The last I saw you, Kyrie, you worked for Toborne. And worst of all, you stole from me," Lady Shey said.

Kyrie looked hurt. "Aye, but it was Toborne who made me do it. Anyway, don't dwell in the past. I have come to bring you some news I have come across."

"Come across? News has come to you while you are trapped?"

Gondrial began to stir awake before Kyrie could answer.

"Oh no you don't," Kyrie said and cast the point of his stick at him. "Sleep, you drunken oaf." Gondrial's head fell back to the pack he was using as a pillow.

"I remember when you taught me that spell," Shey said.

"Aye, you were just a little sprite of a girl, wide-eyed, and curious." His smile faded into a grim expression. "The enemy has been busy. They are planning something big. The Sacred Land is the least of your problems. You should get back to Lux Enor as soon as you can. I have heard stirrings here and there that something is about to happen in the capital. You might not want to be so far away when it all goes down."

"What have you heard?" She paused, "While you have been trapped somewhere."

"I sense you are dwelling on that fact. There are rodents, bugs and all sorts of creepy crawly things everywhere, even where I am trapped. They tell me everything. You think so swallow."

"Okay, eww, but go on."

He started fidgeting with the fire again, "There are whispers that Drakkius is going to make his move and the council members are all behind him. That's all I know. I wish I knew more."

"I'll get myself back the capital as first thing in the morning."

Kyrie stood again, craned his head as if he were about to say something else and then he nodded, "Just get back there and be careful. I must go. I have been away too long."

"Yes, you have."

He looked at her inquisitively, "Oh, yes, away from you too long as well. I meant...oh never mind. I will be leaving now. Bye" He waved the stick and was gone with a pop and a flash of light.

The light of day had barely made its presence known when Shey awoke to Gondrial shaking her awake. "Gondrial, it's barely morning."

"Up and at 'em. You don't want to stick around this place any more than you have to do you?"

"No, I suppose not. It's just that I didn't get as much sleep as you. And by the way, you *do* snore!"

Gondrial curled his lower lip, "Hmm, funny no one else has ever said anything about it."

Shey smirked and then began gathering up her things before digging into her pack for her cup. She went to the fire where Gondrial had a pot of dark liquid boiling and poured herself some. "Good, you made some Bittering Tea."

"Aye, help yourself, it's mountain grown. I bought the beans in Brookhaven the last time I was through there as coincidence would have it."

"So, you will be heading back there?"

"Aye, I will, but I am in no big hurry. I might make a few stops along the way."

Shey blew into her cup before taking a sip, "was that supposed to be a crack about midnight meetups?"

Gondrial was shocked, "You are surprisingly vulgar-minded for one possessing the title of Lady."

"Well? Look who I have to work with, and don't act so shocked, I know you aren't."

"For your information, I did not mean I was going to see any womenfolk along the way. I have some errands to run for Enowene. She asked me to do her a few favors."

"Oh, and if there are women along the way too?"

"I will give them your kindest regards."

CHAPTER 3

REIGN IS FALLING

Lady Shey was in a somber mood when she returned to Lux Enor from The Sacred Land. The castle of the highlord looked devoid of life as she approached. The parapets were unmanned, as they were far too often, and the gates were guarded by a single century, half of the sconces and a quarter of the braziers remained unlit, and the towers were dark. Shey entered through the main gates with a nod at the guard and arrived at the stables where an eager stable boy took her horse. At least the stables were well manned. No one greeted her in the castle hallways and corridors. She had to gauge the time of night several times to make certain she was not arriving later at night then she thought. On a whim, she decided to check the rest of the castle. She couldn't shake the ominous feeling of dread building inside of her; it swelled as soon as she cleared the castle walls at the center of the capital city of Lux Enor. Her mood quickly descended as soon as she entered the throne room. Highlord Rastafin Stowe was shouting at a servant for, no doubt, some minor infraction. She tried to slink in without him noticing her, but of course, he looked her way after just one step.

"Where have you been, my lady? I have needed your counsel for two days."

Lady Shey put back her shoulders and walked up to the throne with her head held high. "I told you, my lord. I went to the Sacred Land to investigate the reports of strange activity, remember? I went at the behest of Master Ianthill of the First Trine."

"I'm not sure I like your tone, *Lady Shey*," he said.

"I meant no disrespect, my lord. Forgive me." She bowed slightly.

"That's better. Now, what did you find out?" He leaned back on his throne. "Hmm? Anything interesting?"

"In the two days I investigated, I found nothing." She lied. "I saw absolutely nothing out of the ordinary. It was just as barren and desolate as always. I think the reports came from men with too many nights of loneliness, too much drink, and amazingly overactive imaginations."

"Is that so?"

"Yes, it is so, sire, the Sacred Land is nothing but a desolate wasteland full of nothing of consequence."

"Well, I'm not sure what you expected to find. I could have told you it was a waste of your time and saved you the trip." His tone was nearly infuriating, but Shey kept calm.

"Aye, your majesty."

In the meantime, I have been without my advisor. I have a good mind to have the treasurer dock your pay." He pointed his finger derisively at her.

"You wouldn't. I was in The Sacred Land on official business."

"Tone, my lady." He wagged his finger at her again. "And I certainly would."

"Sorry, my lord." She went to stand beside his throne. "You needed my counsel?" She decided to change the subject. "I offer it to you now. What is the issue?"

"No, I should think not. You're dismissed." He made a dramatic point to look away from her. "But no more excursions, official or otherwise. I want you by my side when I call."

Lady Shey nodded but said nothing, that is, until she was out of earshot, and then she had a few choice words to mutter. It was no secret among those at court that the highlord had other interests in Lady Shey, but she had no interest in him. Besides the fact that he was married, and his wife mysteriously disappeared, there was also the matter of his disposition, which was less than desirable. Lady Shey had more than once wondered why the Silver Drake had chosen him to lead the five kingdoms. It was also rumored that she had partaken in an affair with the highlord, a rumor Shey found repugnant and offensive.

Lady Shey was reaching for the doorknob to her private chambers when the servant the highlord had been yelling at earlier in the throne room caught her attention.

"Lady Shey, Lady Shey! Come quickly. They're in the throne room. I must find the master at arms."

"Who? Who is in the throne room?"

"I don't know who they are, but they're after the highlord."

"All right, you go find the man at arms, and I'll go see what's going on in the throne room," Lady Shey said before pushing the servant along. *Why is the man of arms not with the highlord?* She thought.

Lady Shey's chambers were only two hallways away from the throne room. At the last moment, she decided to enter the throne room through the secret side entrance. The doorway from the throne room was designed to be seamless, Shey knew, so she just cracked it open enough to peer through it. Two men wearing leather armor and carrying heavy swords were striding down the main corridor of the throne room. Lady Shey was confused. From the way the servant was carrying on, she thought the men had already confronted the highlord. The man walking in front unsheathed his sword and pointed it at the startled highlord.

Lady Shey abruptly pulled the hidden door open, exited the secret corridor, and cast the man's sword from his hand with a wisp of magical essence. He looked at her, cracked a smile, and held his hand out to the spot where his sword clanged on the floor. The sword returned to his hand in an instant. He waved it once above his head, and in a slicing motion, lowered it to the highlord's chest.

The highlord's eyes were pleading. "Do something, Lady Shey!"

"Stop your pathetic pleading!" the man commanded.

Lady Shey drew in essence and prepared to unleash it on the highlord's attacker. She could tell by the man's actions that he could feel her draw in essence. He immediately thrust his sword into the highlord's chest before Shey could unleash it. At the same time, the highlord was gasping for breath, Shey let loose her spell. The highlord's attacker blew back into the marble walls with tremendous force. The second attacker, smaller than the first and dressed in black, reacted. He expertly lobbed two daggers at her. Daggers she knew how to block well. With one fluid motion, she waved her forearm, and the daggers missed her, bouncing off the marble walls behind her.

The first man, now recovering from her attack, rejoined the fight. Shey felt the invisible essence strike her chest. A moment later, she was on the floor. She had her eyes shut, reeling from the pain, but she could hear the commotion of the man at arms and his men entering the throne room. They temporarily commanded the attention of the attackers.

Shey took the opportunity to go to the highlord. His body was limp; his eyes were open, frozen in the visage of terror. She reached down and closed his eyelids.

The man at arms came up behind her. "How is he? I sent one of my men to fetch the clerics on the way here."

"He's gone. There was nothing I could do. The sword must've pierced his heart; he died instantly," Shey said.

"That's unfortunate," the man at arms said.

Lady Shey had no love for the highlord, but she was still sympathetic. "It's more than unfortunate this man lost his life. Where in Fawlsbane's name were you? Why were you not here where you belong?"

"I meant no disrespect, my lady. I was called away. The highlord sent me out. I left two men here." He glanced around. "Although I do not see them now."

"Did you capture the assassins?"

"They are both wounded, but they still managed to slip away. I have men on it."

Shey nodded and then reached under the highlord's shoulders. "Here, help me get him into a more dignified position."

The man at arms grabbed ahold of the highlord's feet and helped Lady Shey stretch him out flat on the marble floor.

"Find something to cover his body. I will return in a moment. I have to alert the King's Council and fill them in on what has happened. If you can manage to stay here." The man looked at her sheepishly.

Lady Shey left the man at arms barking out orders to his men and securing the highlord's body. She made an effort to hurry to the King's Council chamber. With the highlord gone, they would need to decide on a ward to handle day-to-day affairs until the Silver Drake could select a new leader. She entered the council chamber to find the five men sitting around a wooden table, locked in debate. They abruptly stopped talking when she entered.

"What is the meaning of this interruption?" a man with dark hair barked at her.

"Forgive me, Lord Drakkius, but the highlord is dead. He has been murdered. The man at arms is with him now. His men fought with the assassins, but they got away. He has men chasing after the perpetrators."

One of the council members, a man named Yarbrough, stood up. "Where was the man at arms when these perpetrators entered the throne room?"

Lady Shey was shocked. "I don't believe I said it happened in the throne room, Councilman."

The councilman winced. "I only assumed . . . Where else would it happen?"

"Indeed, where else?" She immediately knew her life was now in danger. *Perhaps if I let him get away with the blunder, I can investigate what really happened*, she thought. They were in on it. It was obvious to her now. "What are your orders?"

Drakkius stood from his chair. "You will investigate these assassins. Go check if the highlord's guards have captured them. Find out what you can and report directly to me in the throne room."

Lady Shey bowed. "As you command, Lord Drakkius." She turned and left the council chamber. "Time to leave," she said to herself. She went to her chambers to get a few things.

While she was hastily packing, she accessed a secret panel under her desk where she kept an emergency requisition for a coach and team of horses. She clutched the paper and threw her good cloak over her arm to hide it. She managed her two bags with her free hand and headed for the stables.

CHAPTER 4

LEAVE-TAKING

L ady Shey entered the stables carrying her two bags. She spotted the stable master giving orders to a stable hand hitching up the carriage she planned to requisition. She disliked speaking with the stable master because he smelled of horse and his rotten teeth made his breath horrendous. His slovenly appearance completed his unpleasant presence. After he noticed Lady Shey was near, he advanced toward her, approaching entirely too close to her face.

She handed him the requisition and held her breath, so she wouldn't have to smell the barrage she knew was about to come.

"Do you already have someone in mind as a driver?" the stable master inquired. "I have a few drivers available. I just need to know your requirements."

Lady Shey put her two bags in front of her to distance herself from him. "My requirements?"

"Aye, a solid driver with experience, or a man who can get things done, a sword carrier, perhaps?"

"You have someone like that?"

"I do. He's a bit jumpy. I think he served in a war for some foreign land at one time or another, but he is good with a sword if you need a strong arm." The stable master rubbed his chin. "He's a handy man to have around; he even stopped a payroll robbery for me once."

"Yes, I require someone like that, please."

"I'll warn you, he isn't much to look at, but he knows how to get the job done." The stable master reached down, took Lady Shey's bags, and tossed them on top of the carriage to be secured.

"You've already sold me on him," She cleared her throat and wagged her finger toward the rear of the coach. "Uh, I would rather you put those bags in the storage trunk if you don't mind; I wouldn't want them to get wet if we run into foul weather."

"Oh, sorry, my lady, I forget these royal carriages have trunks strapped to the rear." He sported a rotten-toothed grin. "Force of habit." He motioned to the stableman on top of the carriage to toss the bags down to the rear of the coach. "Oh, by the way, I was sorry to hear about the highlord. I heard tell you were fond of him. It might be none of my business, but some say that . . ."

"You are correct, sir, it is none of your business. However, I assure you the highlord and I were never in amorous relations, or any other relations for that matter, other than the business of the kingdom."

"Forgive me, my lady."

"You are forgiven. Now, if you'd be so kind as to find the driver you spoke of, I shall be on my way."

"Aye, I shall return shortly."

Shey froze. How did he know about the highlord so fast? Either he knew something, or perhaps news traveled fast. Of course, all the commotion would have many tongues wagging; she conceded that much.

She nervously waited in the coach for quite a while. As she watched the passersby, she became increasingly anxious and finally decided to find the stable master. She stepped outside of the coach and came face-to-face with a large man carrying a sword and a bow. She was startled by his ominous appearance. She struggled not to stare at the scar over his left eye or his scarred left ear. She focused instead on his jet-black hair, which was in recede.

"Something wrong, my lady?" he said.

"Um, no, you startled me, that's all. I wasn't expecting to step from the coach into someone."

"I'm your driver. Name's Rodraq."

"Nice to meet you, Rodraq. My name is Shey Namear." She held out her hand, and Rodraq lifted his sword and bow.

"Oh, yes, of course," Shey said lowering her hand. "I'll see myself into the coach."

Rodraq nodded and stowed his sword and bow near the driver's seat of the coach. He hesitated before he climbed onto the seat himself. "Where we headed, my lady?" He said before the door closed.

She pushed open the door a little more to answer, "Through the Sacred Land to Old Symbor." She said pulling the door closed. It clanked shut and then popped open again. "I think the latch might be stuck."

"Here, let me, my lady."

Lady Shey sat back into the luxuriously cushioned seat. "Thank you."

"Aye, my lady." He shut the door behind her and secured the door latch. "We after the high lord's killers?"

The hair on the back of her neck pricked up, "Why do you ask?"

Rodraq shrugged, "You're leaving the capital. No one else would be allowed to leave under the circumstances." The coach tilted to the left as he climbed aboard.

"Let me put it this way, the sooner you get us out of Lux Enor, the better."

"Aye, my lady." He snapped the reins, and the coach lurched.

"Rodraq."

"Aye, what is it, my lady?"

"We will be stopping to pick up a passenger a few miles south of the city, an elven woman. There is a copse of trees not far from the main road; she'll be waiting for us there. You can't miss her."

"Is she important to the investigation?"

"Aye, she is. Forgive me for asking, but where do your loyalties lie, by the way?"

"I'm with you, my lady, I like seeing justice done; that's all."

"Very well. Pick up the elven woman. She is vital to the investigation."

"Aye, my lady. I'll keep my eyes open for her."

The coach rode comfortably along the rutted streets of Lux Enor. Lady Shey sank back into her padded seat. *So, this is how royalty rides*, she thought. She had almost allowed herself to fall asleep when Rodraq pulled the reins on the four white horses to stop the coach. A few moments later, she heard the familiar sound of the metal steps and the coach door opened to admit her elven passenger.

"It's good to see you—" Shey began.

"No, my lady, careful with your greeting. I am an unassuming traveling companion. Simply call me Sylvalora, dear. In fact, why don't you call me Sylvalora until I tell you otherwise." She winked at Lady Shey.

"Of course, I understand." Shey reached out her hand to help Sylvalora take her seat. "But it is good to see you."

"And you, my dear. It has been entirely too long since our last meeting."

Rodraq peered through the coach door. "On now to Old Symbor, my lady?"

"Old Symbor?" Sylvalora asked.

"That would be fine, Rodraq," Shey said.

"Aye." He put the coach in motion once more.

Shey crossed her hands on her lap, "I hope you're not easily frightened, Sylvalora. There have been reports coming from The Sacred Land of late. I even went there recently myself and found out a bit more than I bargained for."

"I know you're not serious. I've never been easily frightened, and I don't plan to start now. You had best keep any revelations you may have learned to yourself for the time being until I deem it safe for us to converse."

"Aye." Shey clamped her lips closed.

"Good. Let me know if we run into any patrols of Defenders. I should like to have a word with them."

"I'm sure they'll stop us after we enter The Sacred Land." Shey heard the sharp crack of the reins, and the coach lumbered forward a bit faster. "So, Sylvalora, I was surprised to get your message." She tapped her temple. "Does your wanting to join me have anything to do with the highlord's death?"

Sylvalora grinned, "I have an interest. I know what you're getting at, and no, the Silver Drake probably will not be choosing a new highlord anytime soon."

"Oh, and why is that?"

"The Silver Drake is inaccessible at the moment."

Lady Shey nodded. "Well, I certainly hope the Silver Drake does a better job of choosing a highlord than it did last time."

"Highlord Stowe had his merits."

"Aye, and he kept them where no one could find them."

"Amusing. No wonder you got along together so well." She gazed around the coach, "I see you have a royal ride. You must have been in good standing with him indeed."

"I must keep up appearances. I am on official business, and the kingdoms respond better to their own. If I pulled up to a palace in a normal, mundane carriage, they wouldn't even admit me."

"It isn't always the material wealth, my dear, sometimes it's the richness in the soul of the person."

"Well put, but this lavish coach will help, you'll see. I have dealt with these petty kings and queens before. They understand money and affluence above all else."

"If you say so, dear, but remember, sometimes people will surprise you." She glanced about, "I assume the birds have flown then?"

"To all the kingdoms by now. They will arrive long before we will. The news will be out soon."

"At least we are getting away before anyone has time to question you."

"Yes, well," Shey adjusted herself in her seat to get more comfortable. "How long that will last is yet to be seen. Are you ready for my news?"

"Hold on a moment," Sylvalora said. "Let me secure the coach." She closed her eyes for a moment. A wave of blue flame covered them and sealed the inside of the coach. "All right, we can speak freely now."

"The Sacred Land is reawakening, but you already knew this, or you would not be here right now. Am I correct?"

"You are correct. What else do you know about it? Why are we really going to Old Symbor?" Sylvalora asked.

"Toborne. When I was an apprentice, he and Morgoran used to experiment with essence and little jade figurines, remember?"

"I was there. I remember."

"The highlord used to keep several of these statuettes on a table near the throne for decoration. After he was assassinated, I noticed they were gone. They were there when I left him for my chambers. The assassins took them. The highlord just liked them because they were intricately carved depictions of elven maidens. He had no idea what they really were, and I liked having them close where I could keep an eye on them."

"So, you are hoping to find a clue about them beneath the White Tower?"

"It was the last place I saw them after Toborne experimented on them. I wonder if there are any more of them left in the basement." She cleared her throat.

"Do you think it was Drasmyd Duil who did this to the highlord? If so, who would be able to control them? They can't think and act on their own someone would have to direct them, dissidents, who have obtained the spells?"

"No, the highlord's council had him assassinated. I'm fairly certain of that. Since there was no smell to the supposed Drasmyd Duil, they had to be just an illusion. The council wanted us to believe it was dissidents, people unhappy with his rule, but it wasn't. They got rid of him for their own benefit and continued on."

"Don't jump to conclusions. You need proof."

Which is why we are headed to the white tower. I am playing a hunch."

"Hunch?"

"Drasmyd Duil stink, remember? Their smell always gives them a way. I think that their appearance was a clever ruse. The council knew there would be no panic or question of their power after dissidents had the highlord assassinated as long as they were still holding the reins of government."

"That's absurd. What would they have to gain? They already have the power. Besides, they would never have let you leave the capital."

"They don't know I suspect them," Shey continued. "But I know they did it because those corrupt idiots are under the control of dark forces, forces who want to control the Sacred Land when it comes back. I know their type, and from what I learned from my trip to the Sacred Land, they are trying to smoke out the opposition so they can eliminate it."

"What opposition?"

"The descendants of the Battlefield. The legacy of the First Trine."

"But again, that would include you."

"I know; now you see why I had to leave Lux Enor."

Won't they notice you are missing and send someone after you."

"Not necessarily. They will only send someone after me if they think I'm a threat. I think they will see my escape as merely me being naïve. Lady Shey is running out to investigate a death she has no clue about. If anything, I think me leaving will give them a false sense of security."

"I see; they will think you're running in the wrong direction chasing phantoms."

Shey nodded, "Drakkius will think he has the upper hand. He might even send someone out to misdirect me; to keep me occupied and away from Lux Enor and away from the real assassins."

"And you are the one who is misdirecting. Where are these descendants?"

"The Jagged Mountains, a village called Brookhaven."

"All of them?"

"I don't know. I guess we'll find out."

Sylvalora sat back in her seat and slouched, "Well, I'll certainly be keeping my eye on you. I think your plan is viable, but it relies on a lot of speculation and assumption."

"You should trust me more, I think."

Sylvalora smiled and closed her eyes.

CHAPTER 5

DEFENDER PATROL

S hey could see the bleak, barren plains and dead forests of The Sacred Land appearing in the distance. Low grey clouds began to accumulate the closer she traveled toward the border villages. Small dwellings were scattered along the edge of the devastated terrain, many in disrepair. Shey felt the familiar oppression, and a general feeling of despair, which always pervaded her psyche when in proximity to the dead land, as the edges of the Sacred Land drew closer. She tried to remember the names of the border villages, but she couldn't recall many of them. They changed and shifted populations and names too many times over the years. The road became rough from mud hardening into ruts. The coach lurched and bounded. She was about to tell Rodraq to take it easy when she felt the coach begin to slow.

Sylvalora slept opposite her. She was stretched out across the whole of the coach bench. Shey wondered briefly how the elvish woman could sleep during such a rocky and jolting ride.

"My lady," Rodraq called down from the driver's seat. "We are approaching a group of men on the side of the road. They appear to have injured among them, but I can't be sure from this distance."

"What colors do they display?"

"White, gold, and red, if I am seeing them correctly."

"Defenders' colors. Most likely a patrol," Shey said.

"This far from The Sacred Land, my lady?"

"We're not that far from the villages. If they have injured men, they may have moved away from the borders to tend to them."

"My lady?"

"Defenders have healers, and they can't use healing magic in the Sacred Land. Stop beside them. Sylvalora and I wish to talk to them."

"Aye, my lady," Rodraq said. When they moved closer to the men, he reined the coach to a stop and hurried down from the driver's seat. He lowered the steps and opened the coach door for Lady Shey.

Shey carefully approached the Defenders. They did have wounded with them. "I am Lady Shey from Lux Enor. Who is in charge here?"

A fierce Defender stood up and brushed off his uniform. His features were chiseled and seasoned, his face wind-bitten. "Our commander was killed near the border villages. I am Juran, the senior-most officer."

"I bid you greetings, Juran. We mean to travel through the border villages. What news do you have of the place?"

"If any other but you asked me, I would turn them away quick as a wink and send them back to where they came. The border villages are being evacuated as we speak. The Sacred Land is giving up her dead from the War of the Oracle. It isn't safe. It puzzles me how the dead from a war fought so long ago on this soil could suddenly return from the shadows, but I have seen it, my lady, I have seen the dead rise and roam."

"I do not doubt you."

"Have you come to perform some sort of magic and put them back where they bloody well belong?"

Shey sighed, "I wish I could say yes, but I am here for a different reason. I am aware of the trouble here, and I assure you I will do what I can." She tried to make her voice as sympathetic as possible. "I am passing through on my way to Old Symbor."

"Old Symbor, well then, I might warn you not to travel through the villages."

"Oh, and why is that?"

"A wielder of your renown might find it interesting to know that there is a rumor of a young boy in one of the border villages who is keeping the walking dead at bay. They say he has the sight of the Oracle himself."

"A seer?"

"As I hear it, my lady."

"I take it you know who I am?"

"Aye, Lady Shey. You are well known amongst the Defenders of The Sacred Land. I knew who you were the minute you said your name."

"Very well, Juran. In which village is this young seer rumored to reside?"

"The village of Valwall, my lady." He swallowed hard, "My lady, you aren't thinking of going there and seeking this boy out? I am trying to warn you off."

"It may be important, Juran, and you asked if I were here to help. I would say it would be my duty to investigate this boy, wouldn't you?"

"What is your plan? If he is the cause of all this, he must be a demon. How will you halt the demon's power to force the dead to the surface?"

Lady Shey peered down the road to the Sacred Land, "It isn't demons. The Sacred Land was stripped of its magic by overuse of essence. The mistake was burying the dead there. You said the boy is a seer and holding the dead at bay. He isn't the cause of the dead rising, but he might be just as dangerous."

"My lady?"

"The Sacred Land is rejuvenating its power. Like when you burn a dead field of grass, and it comes back green and vibrant. It just took a lot of years for the Sacred Land to make its comeback. The dead buried there are being animated by the process, or so I've been told. The Seer might be a product of the Oracle, the one who caused the war in the first place. The seer might be a rejuvenation of the Oracle's power."

"Aye, I believe the magic is coming back, but the dead rising has nothing to do with the magic returning, you are mistaken."

"Oh, do you know something I don't?"

"Rumor is that a man came using the old ways of the necromancer. He wielded Interminis, the sword of the dead! He thrust the fell blade into the heart of the Sacred Land, and the dead came. It is the power from the underworld! It is demons, my lady!"

"Interminis? I thought that sword was only a legend, like the dragon sword. I forget what it's called."

"What else but the sword of death could have raised the dead? Are there necromancers roaming once more?"

She could see the soldier was truly scared, "We will look into all possibilities, but for now do not go about spreading these rumors; they are only rumors, after all, unless you have proof?"

The soldier nodded his head.

"If the boy is holding off the dead, he is something else. Try not to spread more panic than we already have. I need you to keep the news, or rumors, of this boy quiet until I have a chance to investigate. Can you do that for me?"

"Aye, my lady."

"Good."

Shey thanked the soldier and returned to her coach. She peered up at her driver, "Get us to Valwall, Rodraq."

"Aye, my lady." He jumped down to raise the steps after Shey entered the coach.

She sat down and eyed Sylvalora, who stared back at her grimly from the opposite seat. Sylvalora's grim expression changed to concern. "The Oracle reborn?"

The coach moved forward.

"I certainly hope not. Could the renewal of The Sacred Land also bring back the Oracle?"

"Who knows? This is the first time anyone has ever seen such a place as The Sacred Land regenerate. If the Oracle foresaw that he would be reborn, it would explain his disappearance during the War. The ranks of wielders have all but been wiped out due to the law against magic. Mindwielders are almost nonexistent. It would be a superb time for him to come back. There is almost no one left to oppose him."

"There is, but it's a long shot at best. After we investigate this child seer, we will need to continue to the White Tower in Old Symbor. I remember my friend Marella and I came across some old books of prophecy in the archives when we were girls."

"Prophecy! Merely fairy tales and fiction," Sylvalora scoffed. "I doubt those books have anything of use in them."

"Perhaps not, but it's not the prophecies I am concerned about. I want to look up the legends of the Smiths. There were some important named swords forged in antiquity. I remember reading about them in those dusty old books, and I think Interminis was one of them."

"The sword of the dead?" Sylvalora said, "It's only a legend. I don't remember it being used in the War of the Oracle. The wielder could have raised the dead to fight, and none of that happened."

"What else do you know about it?"

"No more than you."

"There is also Toborne's old laboratory chambers beneath the tower. He was fond of collecting stories and prophecies. He may have left something behind in his private library. He collected the ramblings of the seers of old and some of the Oracle himself."

"I don't know Shey," She said. "Those books would have to be magically sealed to have survived this long. I know Enowene protects the tower archives, but who protects Toborne's books?"

"I suppose we will find out," Shey answered. "You're right; they may all be dust by now. I still want to go down there and take a look around."

"You can try, but I think it's a waste of time."

"It's worth a shot." She was annoyed at Sylvalora's pessimism, "Weren't you sleeping!"

Sylvalora smirked and nodded, lying back on the cushions, "Wake me up when we get there."

The first of the border villages did not appear out of the ordinary until Lady Shey's coach entered the wooden gates. The people scrambling about were not going about their daily tasks but were instead preparing to leave. Wagons were piled high with belongings, and families packed themselves into the fold of the wagons wherever they could. The streets were in chaos, with men directing their wagons around others that were stalled for one reason or another. Shey ordered Rodraq to continue through the village without stopping. She and Sylvalora already knew why the villagers were leaving.

"What are we getting ourselves into?" Lady Shey asked Sylvalora. "It's worse than I thought."

"Yet, it could be worse," Sylvalora said. "As chaotic as it seems, at least no is no one is getting trampled."

"I take little consolation in that," Shey said.

"We will need to push onward. Once we get deep into The Sacred Land, I'm sure we can find the cause of the danger and stop it. If we are lucky, maybe we can avoid trouble altogether."

"Aye, I will keep telling myself that."

Sylvalora breathed a sigh, "Try to remain positive, dear."

"There's positive, and then there's insane blindness to the facts."

"Oh, and which one are you subscribing to right now?"

Lady Shey ignored the questioning comment, "The next village is situated directly on the border. Do you think we should avoid it and go around?"

Sylvalora glanced out the coach's window at some of the villagers scrambling to leave. "It's difficult to say. We would have to leave the coach and travel on horseback if we did. I think for now we should travel the road and hope for the best. We don't know what we're going to meet out there, whether it be by road or traveling in the wild."

Shey nodded, "That's thinking positive."

Sylvalora gave her an icy stare.

Shey lowered the small window on the coach door. "Rodraq, continue on the road to the next village."

"Aye, my lady. You do realize the next village is Valwall, do you not?"

"Understood. Yes, take us to Valwall." Shey sat back in her seat, "I hope you're right, and this isn't as bad as it seems."

Sylvalora looked away, absently peering out the window, "I *try* to remain positive. No matter how bad things get, they can always be worse."

CHAPTER 6

VALWALL

When the coach came within sight of the village of Valwall, Rodraq commanded the horses to halt. Shey heard him set the brake and climb down. The coach door opened, and Rodraq lowered the steps. "You might want to see this," he said.

Shey stepped out of the coach and helped Sylvalora down. They peered into the distance at the medium-sized village. Even though the sun had not yet set, the village was surrounded by the abominations of unlife. The dead of the battles and atrocities of the War of the Oracle had risen, and they walked, hovered, and floated around the perimeter of Valwall.

"Are they looking to get in or is something holding them back and keeping them out?" Shey asked.

Sylvalora squinted to get a clearer look. "I would say something is keeping them out."

"Something in that village is attracting them," Rodraq said, "something they are trying to get at."

"Which means we should be able to ride past them and enter the village unmolested. But, just to be safe, wait until there is a break in the line around the entrance and then drive the coach through," Shey suggested. "That way if the abominations do come after us, they will not be able to follow us into the village."

"A wise plan," Rodraq agreed.

"Let's get in there and find this seer boy. I have a feeling he is both the source of the attraction and the force keeping those things at bay," Sylvalora said as she stepped back into the coach.

Shey pulled up the hem of her dress and stepped onto the first step. "Drive on, Rodraq. Be as cautious as you can."

"Aye, my lady. I will see us safely through the gates."

As Lady Shey had commanded, Rodraq waited at a distance from the gates until there was a break in the line before taking them forward into the village. Once they had passed the gates, they were safe. The creatures surrounding the city could not enter. Lady Shey changed from her dress into breeches and climbed up the outside of the coach to join Rodraq in the driver's seat. The village seemed abandoned as they traveled its dirt and cobblestone streets. Most of the buildings were in disrepair and appeared to have been assaulted of late. Windows were broken, and doors were torn from their hinges.

"Go to the village square, Rodraq. The people might have relocated to a central, defensible location," Lady Shey suggested.

Rodraq complied and took the coach down what he thought might be the quickest path to the middle of the village. "The sun is on its way home," he pointed out. "We will be here, stuck in the dark."

"As long as the abominations stay outside, I am not too worried about spending the night here."

The coach rounded the final corner and entered the village square. At the center, sprawled out and tied to scaffolding was a young, blond-headed boy of about ten seasons. Strewn out around on the ground before him were the villagers. They appeared from Lady Shey's angle to all be dead, save for the boy who was moaning.

Rodraq reined in the horses. "What in the name of evil happened here!"

Lady Shey climbed from the coach and went to the nearest villager. She put her ear close to the woman's mouth and listened. "She's not dead. I hear her breathing." She moved to the next man and found the same. "They are not dead . . . yet. Rodraq, check the others while I see about the boy."

The big man set the brake and climbed down from the coach. He went to the closest villager and began turning over bodies, checking for signs of life.

Sylvalora followed Shey to the boy. "Don't take him down yet. We need to find out what happened here first."

"I will not leave a boy hanging up like a scarecrow in a field!"

"Leave him, Shey! Now you listen to me this time. We don't know what is happening here."

"I know they are abusing this child!" Shey reached up and severed the rope holding him with one of the daggers she carried. He slumped down into her arms, and she helped him lie down on the wooden platform.

Sylvalora stood over Lady Shey's shoulder. "A fool thing to do when we know so little."

Lady Shey ignored her.

"My lady, this villager is conscious." Rodraq was helping a young woman walk to where Shey tended to the boy.

The girl looked at the boy and started clawing at Rodraq. "No, get me away from him. Put him back up where he belongs." She was terrified, and Rodraq let her go when she feebly tried to pull away from him. She took two steps and collapsed to the ground. Rodraq went to her aid.

"Put him back where you found him," Sylvalora said, expressionless.

"I will not!" Lady Shey said.

"The girl is dead," Rodraq announced. "I think she may have been frightened to death."

Lady Shey looked up from the boy to see what Rodraq was talking about. The girl pushed herself up behind him. "She isn't dead. She is standing up behind you."

Rodraq turned around. "Missy, I thought you stopped breathing." He reached for her. She whirled around in a singular, fluid motion. She leaped at Rodraq, screeching. Her mouth opened wide, too wide. The sides of her mouth ripped, and blood ran down her chin as she gurgled and spat, trying to get at him. He reached for his sword, pushing her away with his free hand. He pulled his sword free and hacked the creature's arm off as she reached for him again. He raised his sword above his head and brought it down at an angle, slicing through the former girl. Once she fell, he finished her off.

Shey looked at the boy. He was moaning and moving his head side to side. "They are coming for me," he whispered.

"Prepare yourself, Rodraq," Lady Shey said. "I think we unleashed the creatures outside the gates."

Sylvalora took the initiative and grabbed the boy. "Help me get him back up on the scaffolding."

Lady Shey reluctantly helped the elven woman put the boy back where she had found him. "This is so barbaric, Sylvalora. We are supposed to be civilized people."

"There is no civility among the dead, Sheyna, nor is there reason, compassion, or empathy."

The boy cringed as Sylvalora pulled the ropes tightly. Shey had to turn away. When she opened her eyes, the villagers were writhing around. She looked again at the boy. She felt essence moving around her.

"He is drawing in essence!" Sylvalora said.

"I think he is taking the life-force from the villagers!" Shey said.

Sylvalora moved to take action. She held up her hands, and bolts of lightning came from her palms, striking the boy.

Shey was horrified. "What are you doing? He is a boy!"

Sylvalora let the lightning bolts fall. "Look."

Shey looked at the boy. He appeared unharmed. He was crying as if he didn't know where he was. The villagers who were killed remained where they fell, while the villagers who still lived began to stand.

"What did you do?" Shey asked Sylvalora as she went to let the boy down from the scaffolding again.

"I must have jolted out whatever force was controlling him."

One of the village women approached. She recognized the boy Shey was trying to help. "Get away from him! What are you doing to my son?" She ran up to Shey and yanked her hands away from him.

"He is the young seer is he not?" Shey asked.

The woman took her son down and held him close. "Of course, he isn't. He is innocent. The boys you seek were run out of town. They are rumored to be dead. There is a cabin about a mile into The Sacred Land. If they live, the Defenders guard him there."

"Boys? There are more than one?"

"Aye, they're twins." The woman said.

"What has happened here?" Sylvalora asked.

"We are all trying to leave. The dead from the wars of The Sacred Land have been invading our village with evil. Our children take ill and are tortured. Some even have the nerve to call this land sacred! I spit at the word. The Sacred Land is more forsaken than any land known to me." She took her boy up in her arms. "If you know what is good for you, you will leave this cursed land!" She ran with her boy toward some of the dwellings.

"Looks like we travel into The Sacred Land, then," Lady Shey said, "And go after these twins."

Sylvalora nodded. "Find where Rodraq has gotten off to; I will meet you at the coach."

Shey surveyed her surroundings. *Where has Rodraq gone?* She thought.

CHAPTER 7

SHADOW FALL

A few moments later, Rodraq returned with the men from the front gate. He was covered in filth and sweat from battle. "We dispatched the invaders, my lady." He said in between labored breaths. "The village is safe," Rodraq said.

One of the men with Rodraq sheathed his sword as he approached and extended his hand. "I am Youree, Reeve of Valwall. I don't believe I have had the pleasure."

Rodraq stepped in front of Shey and blocked her from the reeve's access facing the reeve with sword out but pointed downward. "This is Lady Shey of Lux Enor. How dare you speak to her so. You may direct your pleasantries to me."

"Oh, step aside, Rodraq. I have nothing to fear here." Shey stepped around the big man and extended her hand to the reeve. "I am Lady

Shey of the Vale of Morgoran, advisor to Lux Enor." She hesitated. "In fact, I actually only work in Lux Enor; I'm not from there."

The reeve took her hand and kissed it while bowing slightly. "My lady. I have heard of you. Terrible thing, the death of the highlord."

"Indeed, it was, good reeve." Her words tumbled from her mouth, and she shot a glance at Sylvalora, who was chuckling. Shey never could hide her attractions to men from the elven woman.

"So, you are investigating his death here in Valwall?" Youree asked.

Lady Shey chose her words carefully dismissing the momentary thought of saying something about the boy. Instead, she decided she had better stick to her cover story. "I go where the trail of evidence leads me, good sir. It is a coincidence that we travel through your village. We were actually heading for The Sacred Land, to Old Symbor."

"Old Symbor! Why the world would you want to go there? We have been getting reports that Old Symbor is where all this nonsense originated. It is far too dangerous." He paused to take in the full sight of her. "For someone...so delicate and lovely as you."

Shey's face felt hot. He must have picked up on her awkwardness. She decided to be stern and commanding. She wasn't about to let the reeve know she felt some attraction to him, "Good sir don't let my exterior fool you. I can take care of myself." She patted Rodraq's armor. "And I have a fine bodyguard." She took a step closer. There was an uncomfortable silence. Shey decided she needed to break it, "Of course, there is something you can do to help me. You could write me a writ of passage."

"But, my lady, you are the highlord's advisor. You can pass freely."

She shook her head, "The highlord is dead. Besides, even if I can travel freely, it sets a good example for the common folk if I keep to the legalities. Wouldn't you agree?"

"Aye, my lady, I will draft you a writ of passage. Just follow me to my office."

Shey addressed Rodraq. "I am all right here. Go to the coach and prepare to travel into The Sacred Land. Get any provisions we need." Rodraq reluctantly agreed. "And Rodraq, make certain you clean up. You look and smell dreadful."

"Aye, my lady." He sheathed his sword and began muttering under his breath as he walked away.

"Shall we?" Lady Shey held out her arm, and the reeve took it.

Youree's office consisted of a rectangular room with two jail cells connected to the rear. There were two desks, one for the reeve and another for his deputy. He motioned for Lady Shey to sit in a small wooden chair.

"I will stand; thank you."

"Suit yourself." He began drafting the writ.

"I wonder if you might be able to tell me about a boy here recently who is thought by some to be a seer?"

The reeve almost knocked over his ink pot. He stared into Shey's sapphire blue eyes, frozen for a moment in thought. She could tell he was trying to craft his answer carefully. She tried her best to accent her eyes with a demure and feminine gaze. It appeared to work as she saw the man's face soften.

"Aye, we had such a boy here. In fact, there were two, twins I believe."

"Twins," Shey repeated. "Tell me more." She leaned toward him, turning on her charm with a lovely smile.

"The Defenders took them into The Sacred Land, a cabin about a league away on the road to Old Symbor. The last report I got was that they were dead. They were killed by the defenders."

"Defenders do not execute people, certainly not boys. They would find a way to turn them into soldiers. When was this report?"

"Actually, I have it right here." He handed her a piece of parchment.

"It is dated with yesterday's date."

"Aye, I got it yesterday."

"When did your trouble begin?"

He looked thoughtful. "Yesterday. Say, you don't think the two events are related, do you?"

Shey resumed her charm. "I doubt it." She handed the parchment back to Youree. Her handprint was still glowing on it, but she hoped the reeve wouldn't notice it. Negating enchanted parchment was easy. It was some of the first magic she had ever learned.

"Here you go, my lady." Youree handed Lady Shey the writ with his seal, in wax, affixed to it.

"Thank you, my good man." She bowed. "No need to follow me out. I know my way. You have many duties to tend to no doubt."

"Let me get the door at least." The man bounded for the door and opened it. Rodraq had pulled the coach just outside the reeve's office, its wheels clipping and clopping on the cobblestone street before it rolled to a stop.

"Ah, see here is Rodraq with the coach." She stepped out of the reeve's office. "I see you still have not cleaned up," she scolded him.

He grumbled before speaking, "I was told of a natural hot spring just south of town. I thought we might stop there for a bath."

Shey was pleasantly surprised, "Aye, that is acceptable. The gods know I could use a soak too." she said as Rodraq closed the coach door. Sylvalora had lowered the steps and was standing next to them. Shey gave her a quick glance and shook her head. Sylvalora bobbed her head and followed her into the coach. The reeve raised the stairs and gave the door a sharp double pat so Rodraq would know the coach was secure and ready to move out.

"Thank you, Reeve," Shey said through the half-opened side window. He nodded and smiled weakly.

Sylvalora took her familiar place across from Shey, "Well, what was that all about?"

Shey signaled for her to secure the coach as it began to move away from the reeve's office, and Sylvalora complied. Once the spell was complete, she sat back tentatively.

"They are holding the boys at a cabin a league or so into The Sacred Land. I suspect when we arrive there, the Defenders guarding them will be dead or worse, unliving."

"Boys? Plural! What did you find out?"

"The village reeve received a report from the Defenders that the boys were dead. It was enchanted. I suspect it was to mislead the reeve so he would no longer pursue the matter."

"Or it was to mislead him so he would turn away any who asked about them."

"I dispelled the charm."

"Is that it?"

"No, I felt a presence, the one who did the enchantment on the message, I could see them for a moment, and it isn't good. I am willing to wager the boys are alive and they have company."

"Company of the worst kind, I presume?" Sylvalora asked.

"Yes, it's been a while since I have run into one. Do you still remember how to detect them?" Shey asked.

"Drasmyd Duil? Aye, they smell horrible. It's unmistakable."

"Why would they try it? They have not fooled us for several years. They are so easy to detect."

"They have gotten clever since you last saw one. For example, it will probably be disguised as a Defender. One who has recently been in battle; dead soldiers and blood would mask the smell.

"If it killed the other Defender guards, the boys will likely not know about it." Shey put her finger to her temple. "If the seer boys are this important, the Drasmyd Duil may be preparing to take them to Naneden. We should hang back and follow them."

"Do you have a headache?"

Sylvalora rubbed her temple, "A slight one, nothing to worry about. So, what do you want to do about the situation?"

"I think we need to get the boys. I think you should cast an enchantment over them, so they are hidden from magic detection, and we keep them with us."

"You don't think that would be asking for trouble?"

"If they are seers, they may be useful to us."

"Ah, you hope to gain insight. I don't know, Shey. Even with my enchantments, we shouldn't keep them in our company for long. What if their gifts come from the Oracle? What if the Oracle *is* awakening with The Sacred Land? You will have a piece of him traveling around with us."

"We can't let them fall into the enemies' hands regardless. I agree they might be troublesome, but until we find a place to secure them, our best course of defense is to keep them close." She bit her lower lip. "You know, I think the best place for them would be the Vale of Morgoran in the tower. We will keep them with us, under our watchful eyes, until we can make the arrangements."

"Assuming we do find them, both of them," Sylvalora said.

The coach came to a stop, and Rodraq tapped on the door. "We are at the hot springs." He pointed to a wooden building surrounded by trees. A flowing stream ran underneath it.

"I suppose we should make use of the hot springs ourselves," Shey suggested.

"Don't you think our priority should be to get the boys?"

"How long of a bath do you plan to take?" Shey asked.

"I usually soak for a while, dear. You know this."

Shey took out a kit with various soaps and bathing products from the storage space underneath her seat. "Just get cleaned up, and we will be on our way. We can come back for a long soaking some other time." Shey knew Sylvalora really had no intention of delaying them to soak. It was her way of saying she disapproved of the delay but understood the importance of bathing. In her own way, she was testing Shey's resolve.

Sylvalora nodded. "Very well. Do you have any more of that lilac soap I like so much?"

"Of course, I do," Lady Shey said as she stepped down from the coach.

CHAPTER 8

BENEATH THE WHITE TOWER

The cabin, nestled in a small copse of trees, which were dead and devoid of essence, sat just off the main road to Old Symbor. Lady Shey wished she had one of the essence-imbued jade statuettes from which to draw in essence to cast her spells. She was good with her daggers but felt naked without being able to use magic as well. On a whim, she tried to draw in essence. To her amazement, essence did come, but it was shallow, like trying to breathe in an overtight corset. It was not enough power to cast better attack spells. She might be able to cast a small protective shield.

When the coach came to a stop, Sylvalora was the first to exit. She whispered a few words, and a quarterstaff appeared. Lady Shey looked jealously on. "How can you conjure that without essence?"

"It doesn't require essence. It's entirely different magic. I can teach you later if you wish."

"What is it, dragon magic?"

"Aye, and extremely easy to cast." She spun the staff in the air, making it whizz and hum. She stopped with it tucked under her armpit.

"I would like to learn that spell," Shey said.

Rodraq, sword in hand, approached. "Plan?"

Lady Shey squinted at the cabin. "It's difficult to see this far away, but it appears no one guards the outside. I say the direct approach."

"Direct it is!" Rodraq said. He held his sword out and marched up to the door of the cabin. In one mighty kick, he obliterated the front door. Shey and Sylvalora were close on his heels. As suspected, a stench assaulted their senses and two Drasmyd Duil, wings wrapped around their lithe bodies, stood perched over a boy of about ten or eleven years. They snarled and attacked. Lady Shey didn't think; she just launched into her trained dagger attacks. First was spinning eagle talon. She whirled in a circle, bringing both daggers, one after the other, to bear on the first Drasmyd Duil as it unfurled its wings. It screamed as she sliced through the thin, leathery right wing before it could get its arm free to claw at her. She dodged its deadly acidic spit. Rodraq was at her side, running his sword through the creature and slicing up and out. The Drasmyd Duil split in two and collapsed, convulsing on the floor. Both Shey and Rodraq turned to the other creature, but Sylvalora was already pulling her ethereal staff from its eye socket. Her staff morphed into a double-bladed staff, a blade on each end, as she swung it over her head and came down on the creature's shoulder. Its head landed somewhere in the corner. Its body buckled, with black blood shooting from its exposed neck as it fell.

Lady Shey put away her daggers and went to the boy. He looked up at her and smiled. "You have come for me?"

"Aye. Can you tell me your name?"

"My name is Geron. Do you know my mother and father?"

"I don't know. Where are they?"

The boy looked distressed. "I think those black creatures killed them."

Shey felt a jolt of sympathy. "You are safe now. Where is your brother?"

The boy shrugged, "I am alone."

"Oh, I was told there were two of you."

"He went with one of those men in the white cloaks a long time ago. They didn't want us to be together."

"Do you know where they might have taken him or which way they might have gone?"

The boy shook his head.

"No, I don't suppose you would know such things." She said.

"Are all the black creatures gone?"

"Aye, they are. We won't let the bad creatures hurt you anymore." The boy reached up and hugged Shey's neck. Her heart instantly melted. "Come with us. We will protect you."

Geron's blue eyes seemed to sparkle. He nodded and took Shey's hand.

When they got to the coach, Sylvalora began her protection spell to shield Geron from any prying eyes. As the coach pulled away, Geron curled up beside Lady Shey and went to sleep.

Sylvalora tapped her forehead. Shey put her hand over Geron's exposed ear.

"He has taken to you," Sylvalora whispered.

"He has. I must admit, I had not expected him to so quickly. I guess I expected him to be somewhat traumatized."

"He may yet be. We both need to keep our eyes on him."

"Can you make sure he sleeps the rest of the way to Old Symbor?"

"I will," Sylvalora said. "I imagine he needs it."

Lady Shey sat beside Rodraq in the driver's seat as the first glimpse of Old Symbor appeared in the distance. She had moved to the top of the coach to allow Geron to stretch out over the entire length of the coach seat while he slept. The White Tower still stood as the tallest building in Old Symbor. It loomed over the city like a forgotten sentinel, guarding a dead city. Once the Sacred Land had engulfed the city and its surroundings, nothing would grow in the farmer's fields or the peasant gardens. The cattle and sheep ranchers no longer had grassy fields for their animals to graze in, and even the flowers couldn't survive the Sacred Land. They all died out and new plants brought in would soon die after they were planted in the soil. They would not even grow in separate house pots. The city survived on imports for a time before the king of Symboria finally declared that the capital be moved out of The Sacred Land. He declared the southern port city of Paladine to be the new capital, and he renamed it Symbor, after the family name of the king forever relegating this place to be called Old Symbor.

Shey felt overwhelming sadness as they passed through the debris-choked streets. Buildings crumbled and decayed everywhere she looked. She felt a tear roll down her cheek as they passed the ruins of the Sleeping Hound Inn where she had once begged for food from the inn's cook, Ignacio. Her heavy heart did not lighten when they reached the yard of the White Tower of Enowene. The outer wall, where she had taken refuge when she was a little girl, had crumbled completely away. Enowene, the headmistress of the academy within the tower, had long ago moved to the Vale of Morgoran.

"I wonder what we will find within those walls," Shey said to Rodraq.

"Is it even safe to go in there? Judging by the state of the rest of the city, I wouldn't think so," he replied.

"It's safe. Enowene has enchantments in place, at least above ground level. She sometimes returns here from what I understand." Shey pointed to a tiny window at the base of the tower. "It's beneath the tower, where we need to go, that I'm concerned about."

Rodraq brought the coach to a stop. "How long will we be here, my lady? This place is...unsettling."

"At least overnight. There are stables around back for the horses. Enowene has it taken care of by the caretaker of the city. It is likely we will see him sooner or later. I knew him once, long ago in this very city. His name is Dicarion. He can be difficult, so if you see him, be sure to mention that you are here with me." She thought for a moment. "In fact, if you see him and I'm not around, tell him you are here with Sheyna Namear rather than Lady Shey."

Sylvalora climbed out of the coach. "The boy still sleeps."

"We need to go ahead and wake him. Rodraq is about to stable the horses and put the coach away."

Sylvalora went back to the coach to wake Geron, but he came stumbling out, rubbing his eyes before she got too far. "How did you sleep, dear?"

Geron continued to rub his eyes. "Good."

Rodraq snapped the reins, and the coach lumbered on.

Lady Shey approached the heavy wooden door of the tower and produced a key from her pocket. "The enchantments on the tower are weak. The Sacred Land has taken its toll on them since Enowene's last visit."

"I'm surprised they stick at all," Sylvalora said.

Shey inserted the key and turned the lock twice to the left and once to the right while reciting the counterspell. The door creaked open. Shey turned to Sylvalora and Geron. "Come on in. I need to go open the entrance from the stables for Rodraq."

Once inside the tower, memories of times gone by flooded Shey's mind. The foyer looked exactly as it did when Shey was a girl. Enowene had managed to keep it from decaying and deteriorating like the rest of Old Symbor. The marble floors shined brilliantly, and the wooden staircase was polished to perfection.

Sylvalora escorted the boy inside. "Enowene's tower. We will be quite comfortable here." She stepped into the adjoining parlor and opened the firewood cabinet. "Plenty of firewood. When you let Rodraq in, Shey, have him build a fire and light the sconces of the main living areas."

"Oh yes, Rodraq!" Shey said. "I had almost forgotten about him already."

"You can explore and reminisce later, dear."

"You're right. Why don't you go to the kitchens and see about the food stores. Enowene should have an enchantment in place to keep the food fresh there as well."

Sylvalora bent down to Geron. "Hungry?"

Geron nodded, and Sylvalora led him off to the kitchens.

Shey navigated the darkened halls and found the back door. She unlocked it in the same manner as the front door and found Rodraq near the stables talking to someone. The man was too young to be Dicarion. Curious, she went to join them.

"I wasn't aware we were to report back to Lux Enor. To whom were we supposed to send such a message? The highlord is dead," Rodraq was saying.

"The ward of Lux Enor, Sanforth Throu, is temporarily in charge. You send the reports to him, I suppose."

Shey recognized the man when she was close enough. "Lyrrath, the ward of Lux Enor sent you?"

"Ah, Lady Shey." He bowed. "There you are. I was just talking to your manservant."

"I can see that. What about?"

"I traveled here soon after you left. I somehow arrived before you." He looked at her questioningly.

"We were delayed. Go on with your explanation."

"At once, my lady. Aye, it was Ward Throu who sent me to ask you for a report on your progress. Have you discovered the highlord's assassin?"

"It's an ongoing investigation."

"I am to join your search and report back regularly."

"Welcome, then," Shey said. "I am sure we will get along fine as long as you let me conduct the investigation and you stay out of my way."

"Of course, my lady."

"So, they don't trust me then. It was good for me to get out of there when I did."

Lyrrath grinned, "They do not, and yes, it was most wise of you to leave you when you did."

"I thought so." She pointed her right index finger at him. I meant what I said though."

"I wouldn't dream of interfering, my lady," Lyrrath said. "I am here to observe and report."

"I sent Sylvalora to the kitchens. Why don't we go see what she found to eat."

"Shall I bring the food stores from the coach?" Rodraq asked.

"Why don't you."

Rodraq went back to the coach while Lyrrath followed Lady Shey into the tower.

"I look forward to working with you, my lady."

"See if you still feel that way in a few days, Lyrrath. I am not fond of Ward Throu, and I am not particularly happy he has sent you to . . . help me."

"You think me to be a spy for the ward of Lux Enor?"

"Aye, are you not?"

"Certainly not! I am still loyal to you as always."

"We shall see." She led him into the kitchens where Sylvalora was already cooking something. Geron was sitting at a preparation table, drawing with coal and parchment. Rodraq came in with the provisions. Lady Shey began putting out plates and silverware.

"Where are we going to quarter?" Rodraq asked.

"I thought we might stay in the guest quarters here on the first floor. I'm not sure if the rooms upstairs are kept up," Shey answered. "I don't want any light in the windows up there to attract people to us either. I can't imagine what manner of people might be lurking about, evading the Defender patrols."

"If you don't mind, my lady, can you show me to my quarters after supper? I plan to go right to sleep after I get a belly full."

"I will show us all to our quarters. The only one who has had any good sleep lately is Geron, and I hope he is able to sleep through the night."

The boy smiled and nodded that he could.

"Good." She sniffed the air. "That smells divine, Sylvalora. What is it?"

"Pork chops and mashed potatoes."

"There were pork chops?" Shey was surprised they kept.

Sylvalora looked at her as if her answer was obvious. "Magical stores tend to be stocked the best. There is also eggs and bacon for breakfast."

The moon loomed high in the midnight sky when Geron ventured out of his room. Lyrrath watched as the boy moved silently in the shadows. He was about to ask the boy what he was doing out of bed when the moonlight, falling through the windows, illuminated the boy's face as he passed from shadow to light and then back into shadow. Instead of a young boy, the face was contorted into the countenance of a stunted dragon's maw. Red eyes reflected the moonlight like a house cat. A set of bat-like wings appeared, and the boy wrapped them around his body as he passed through the light of another window and back into shadow. Lyrrath sniffed the air. There was no repulsive odor detectable. He knew the boy had not seen him, so he took the opportunity to follow him. From his pocket, he produced a small jade statuette and drew some essence from it, enough to cloak himself in darkness and make himself undetectable as well as give himself vision to see through the darkness. He followed the shadow-lurking creature down stone stairs into the dungeon, still not fully believing what he was seeing.

After dodging some potentially dangerous crumbling stone walls, Lyrrath emerged into a chamber of glass tubes, cauldrons, and rows of old parchment and books. There was a tinge of an enchantment detectable to him, which explained why the laboratory was not covered in layers of dust and why there was no odor of decay from the old parchments and other time-sensitive materials. He could also detect the same magic emanating from some of the parchments on the shelves. The creature he knew as Geron rummaged through some of the contents on a table and directly produced a stone. He held it up to examine it in the small amount of moonlight that streamed through the tiny window at the base of the tower. The creature cackled and wrapped its wings around itself again. Lyrrath moved to get out of its way and inadvertently kicked some of the crumbling stone wall he was standing near. The Shadow Lurker didn't hesitate. It was on him in one leap; wings extended again. The stealth spell Lyrrath had cast dropped.

"You are the one called Lyrrath." The creature spoke with a low, raspy voice.

Lyrrath reached for the statuette in his pocket, but the Shadow Lurker caught his hand. "Aye, I am he. Who are you?"

"I can't kill you. It would draw suspicion." He moved Lyrrath's hand aside. "What are you trying to get at?" He found the statuette. "Ah, you have magic essence stored in this. Is this essence? Your fuel for a spell, perhaps?"

Lyrrath felt the creature draw the essence from the statuette. "What are you doing?"

"Something you will not remember," the creature said. "Ahh, it feels good to touch magic once again. This place is so devoid of it."

Lyrrath tried to struggle free when he felt the creature in his mind.

"Do not struggle. It will be over in a moment, and you will be happily ignorant again."

Lady Shey awoke to the smell of bacon, eggs, and bittering tea. After she tied her hair back and got dressed, she hurried to the kitchen. Geron was there, drawing with coal and parchment again. Sylvalora prepared breakfast over the cooking hearth, and Lyrrath, looking tired with bags under his eyes, sipped on some bittering tea.

"Top of the morning to you all," she said. Geron bolted for her and embraced her in a hug. "Careful you don't get black coal all over me, child."

"Sorry," he said.

"That's all right. Why don't you go wash up for breakfast."

He nodded and ran off. Shey thought she saw Lyrrath cringe when the boy ran past him. "What is the story with you this morning?"

"I didn't sleep well. It's this blighted land—I kept dreaming of black creatures in the night and all manners of horrible things."

"This place can get to you, especially if you are a wielder. The lack of essence around takes some getting used to."

"That must be it. I don't like it. The sooner we leave this place, the better."

Rodraq entered the room. He was dressed in leather and linen. Shey was not used to seeing him out of his armor. "I found a way down into the dungeon. We can go there after breakfast."

"Not me," Lyrrath said. "If you don't mind, I think I would rather stay up here. In fact, I may go back to bed and see if I can catch up on some sleep."

"I think that would be fine," Shey said. "There probably won't be much to observe today."

Lyrrath gave her a slight head nod, "I don't expect there will be.

Shey knew he understood her sarcasm but chose not to play into it as she has hoped he would. She decided to change the subject. "Where did the fresh eggs come from? She asked.

"The caretaker brought them in this morning." He replied. "His chickens are not far from here, apparently."

"Ah, Dicarion, he's a good man. I wonder why he didn't stay? I would have liked to talk to him."

"He didn't say. He dropped off the eggs, told Sylvalora where the bacon was kept, and promptly dismissed himself."

Shey nodded. She could tell something was distressing Lyrrath, but when Sylvalora sat a plate in front of them both, she decided to eat rather than indulge in prodding his feelings.

After breakfast, Rodraq led Shey, Geron, and Sylvalora down a maze of crumbling stone corridors into the dungeon. Shey remembered where to go, and soon they were in the private laboratory and workshop of Toborne.

"What is it we are searching for?" Rodraq asked while picking up a blank piece of parchment, which appeared almost new, on a work table. "This parchment can't be that old."

"It's an enchantment." Shey said, "Everything here is aging at a much slower rate."

"Where's the dust?"

"Another enchantment," She told him.

"We should use these enchantments on other things," Rodraq said.

"They are costly, difficult to cast and wear down very quickly when there is a bunch of people around," Sylvalora told him.

"Oh." He said.

Sylvalora met him at the table. "Let me see that, please." Rodraq handed over the parchment. Sylvalora concentrated on it for a few moments, and writing appeared. "As I expected. It is ancient but also enchanted."

"What does it read?" Lady Shey asked.

"It's part of a journal. I suspect a few pages fell out of a larger volume of notes. Toborne must have removed some of his belongings in haste. This page is written in an ancient language. I can still read some of it. It mentions a village that doesn't exist yet in the Jagged Mountains. There the line of the Ardens will produce one who will possess the power to defeat the Oracle."

"The Oracle. Was this written during the War of the Oracle?" Shey asked.

"There is no way to know." She picked up another page and brought the words out of it. "This one says there are several who will grow up around the one who will aid . . . It trails off there." She turned the page over and looked at some other parchment. "That's all there is, just these two short entries."

"It's a trick," Rodraq said. "That's some pretty relevant and specific stuff to have just fallen from a book.

Shey breathed in. "Well, there is nothing here about Morgoran?"

Sylvalora looked around some more. "No, the rest are just formulas and notes about the jade statuettes." Sylvalora gave Lady Shey a look. "I think you already know what happened to Morgoran and his involvement in Toborne's experiments."

"Aye, I do. I have also hoped his involvement with Toborne was just with essence and the statuettes and not with his darker experiments on dragonkind. It is rumored that Morgoran trapped Toborne's being, his essence, in one of those jade statuettes. I was hoping to find proof."

Geron picked up a piece of parchment from the floor. "Is this one?"

Sylvalora took the parchment from Geron and gave him a friendly rub on the head. "I will look." After a few moments staring at the writing, Sylvalora's face turned grim.

"What is it?" Shey asked.

"I'm not sure you want to know. It might affect you personally."

"If it helps us get closer to the truth, I must know."

"It is a letter between Toborne and the Oracle, Kambor. I would say it was written during the War of the Oracle. Kambor had a dream in a trance where he saw the lineage of Marella destroy him and Toborne both. He is instructing Toborne to kill her. He also talks about a village in the future where this descendant will be born, but the vision doesn't give him the exact location of where the village will come to be built."

"That's obviously a plant," Rodraq said. "Why would he leave that there to be discovered so easily?"

"I don't think it was intentional. In fact, I don't think he left any of this intentionally," Shey said. "He was destroyed before he could come back and retrieve or destroy them. And if his essence is freed and he does come back, it's too late now."

"Someone else might have left it for us then," Rodraq concluded.

"What's our next move?" Sylvalora asked.

Lady Shey seemed to hesitate. "I know where Marella's bloodline resides. She was my best friend, and I wanted to keep them safe. I think it's time to pay them a visit. There is an apothecary there named Sanmir who Ianthill and I asked to keep an eye out on the boys."

"This isn't the first time you have heard of this prophecy, then," Sylvalora said.

Shey shook her head. "No, I was just hoping it wasn't true. Morgoran, in his state now, also predicted it. We will all need a disguise." Lady Shey said. "It's a simple village, and the presence of a lady would draw too much attention.

"Fine, we go there in disguise," Sylvalora said. Rodraq will take us in the coach to Soldier's Bluff, and from there we will ride in disguise. Rodraq will stay with the coach in Soldier's Bluff. His presence would cause a commotion."

Rodraq protested. "I don't think that's wise."

"It isn't The Sacred Land, Rodraq. I won't be needing physical protection. These people aren't accustomed to seeing such a grizzled warrior such as yourself."

Rodraq reluctantly backed off the point.

"There's not much more we can do here, but I will look around some more for good measure," Sylvalora said.

Lady Shey noticed Geron had a big grin on his face. "What are you so happy about?"

"I like to travel, and I like being with you. None of you have mentioned getting rid of me."

Lady Shey took his hand. "Of course we wouldn't get rid of you. What a funny thing for you to say. Come on, we will go upstairs, and you can help me pick out a disguise."

CHAPTER 9

NIGHTMARES

S ylvalora crossed in front of Lady Shey as she guided Geron toward the spiral stairs. "Before you take the boy to find a disguise, might I have a word with you? In private?"

"Of course," Shey said.

Sylvalora escorted Shey into an adjacent room. Shey was a bit concerned and felt her heart race a bit, "What is it?"

Sylvalora looked around and then cast the privacy spell to seal the room. Once she was satisfied their speech was secure, she faced Shey urgently, "Do you remember the portals?"

Shey nodded, "I do a little. Weren't they all destroyed?"

"Mostly, yes, but there is one in this tower. I discovered it this morning when I was looking for the bacon. It's in a room near the basement," She leaned in closer as if someone might hear despite her privacy spell, "and it's intact."

"And?" Shey asked.

"I swear woman, think. You could use it to go ask Morgoran about the situation we're in."

Shey's serious face turned to quiet laughter until she saw that Sylvalora was not smiling. "You can't be serious. The portal has to connect to a counterpart and as you just pointed out they are all destroyed."

"I said no such thing. I said they were mostly destroyed. I happen to know the portal to the Tower of Morgoran is also intact.

"I don't know, Sylvalora, I've never used such magic before. It sounds quite dangerous to me. I mean leaving one point and appearing in the next hundreds of leagues away."

"Oh, pish posh, it's no more dangerous than any other magic you have used. Migarath the Sorcerer invented them, and wielders have used them successfully for centuries. As I remember it, you used one or two in your youth."

"I consider myself wiser now. Besides, they were mostly intact back then. The same magic war that created this Blight put an end to them for a reason."

"If you are concerned about the lack of essence, you can manage them just fine with dragon's magic. They respond to the arcane."

"Oh, Sylvalora, what good would it do anyway? Morgoran is far from coherent. The curse still has him."

"I may have something for that." Sylvalora reached into her pouch, the one she kept dangling from the thin belt around her lithe waist. "Here." She handed Shey a smooth, round stone."

"A Lora Daine?"

"No, it's a Lora Orbius, a dragon eye." Shey shrank back, "What are you backing away for? It's not an actual eyeball! I swear, how old are you?"

"Old enough to know there is no such thing. I have been around longer than I care to admit, and I have never once heard of a Lora Orbius!"

"It's older than even you, Shey. It's extremely rare dragon magic. Its use will temporarily abate Morgoran's madness long enough for you to have a few minutes of coherent conversation." She handed the stone to Shey who looked at it and then relegated it to her pouch.

"You will keep an eye on Geron?"

"Of course, I will don't worry. Everyone will be here and ready to move out when you return. You should be able to go to from tower to tower instantaneously. I should think it wouldn't take you more than a half hour start to finish."

Shey nodded and opened the door to the room instantly negating Sylvalora's spell. Geron was standing beside one of the round windows peering out emotionlessly. Shey looked around but didn't see Lyrrath anywhere.

"He left," Geron said without looking away from the window.

"Why?" Shey asked.

"He just left," Geron said. He craned his head to look at Shey. For the first time since Geron had joined them his strange gaze gave her an uneasy feeling in the pit of her stomach.

"Well, you will need to go with Sylvalora for a while. I need to run an errand."

"Can't I go with you?"

"No child. I won't be long. I promise."

"We will go outside and explore the grounds," Sylvalora said. "It will be fun."

Geron seemed to perk up, "That sounds fun."

"Come along." Sylvalora took his hand and led him to the door. She peered back at Shey once with a sharp cut of her eyes, and a quick nod, beckoning her to go on and find the portal.

Shey complied and looked around for the basement door. She was familiar with the layout of the tower from her childhood. She had spent quite a bit of it exploring the ins and outs of the tower and grounds with her best friend, Marella, but she still needed to orient herself. She found the door and started down the stone steps. She took the torch from the top sconce and went back up the stairs and used the fire from the cooking hearth to light it. Returning to the basement stairs once more, Shey stepped slowly onto each step. She didn't tell Sylvalora, but she knew exactly where the portal was located. She had been in the room before and had even toyed with getting the portal primed once before Enowene caught her and Marella fiddling with it and stopped them.

The dusty floor of the room gave away the fact that Sylvalora had entered it recently. The stone and polished wood of the portal opening looked clean and dust free just as it did all those centuries ago when Shey was a young, naïve apprentice wielder. The archway was large enough for her to walk into without leaning down, although someone a little taller than her would not get through so easily. At first, she tried to draw in essence magic, just to try, but as she expected, there was not enough to get the portal primed. Reluctantly she switched to dragon magic. She could cast the magic because she was connected to the dragons, much the same way the Dragon Knights were. Her heritage allowed her to use it, but she was not very good at it and certainly not comfortable with it at all. She spoke the words in what little dragon speech she knew and to her great discomfort felt her sapphire blue eyes began to burn. She couldn't see them, of course, but she knew they would be an orange-red color to anyone who could. The transformation hurt them and made them water fiercely afterward. She was so bad at speaking ancient dragon that she was surprised to feel her eyes burn and see the stone around the portal lite up with ancient runes, but they did. Under the arches appeared a swirling wind that became infused with a thousand points of light streaking inward. Shey touched a couple of the runes, and the swirls changed colors until she saw the blue and white swirls she knew represented the Tower of Morgoran. Taking a deep breath, she stepped into the swirl. Her stomach went queasy for a moment, and she had the sensation of falling before the familiar walls of Morgoran's tower appeared. She almost lost her breath when she felt the rush of essence magic return to her. She had forgotten what it felt like to be in its presence after spending so much time devoid of its access in the Sacred Land.

The portal room was near the scribe room where Morgoran kept to his bed. It was called the scribe room because the old wizard was surrounded by a group of scribes who scribbled down every word in case some of his prophecies might come true. His curse of clear eyes forced him to see possible futures endlessly. Each decision made would change the possible futures forcing him to see things come to pass and then change. The Silver Drake had cursed him for getting in its way.

Shey stepped into the low light of the scribe room to see Morgoran asleep on his small bed. His breath was a bit labored. She imagined it would be tough to get a good sleep with future visions always present in one's mind. She went to his side and looked at his white-bearded face. He had not changed since she was a young girl, his apprentice. Although they were completely clear now, except for the whites, she could remember the kindness in his blue eyes. They were not as strikingly blue as hers, but they were a pleasant darker blue. She smiled as she positioned her hand just above his face. She wanted to cradle his cheek, but she knew to touch him would probably wake him, and she did not wish to disturb his fitful sleep. There was a slight breeze coming through the open window keeping the room at a pleasant temperature. He was sleeping so peacefully that she decided to go back to the portal and come to see him another day. When she moved to return to the portal room, she noticed the shadow in the corner for the first time. She assumed the figure was one of Morgoran's many caregivers.

"Oh, I'm sorry. I didn't see you there." The figure did not reply. "I will be going. I wanted to check in on him."

"Leaving so soon?" The figure said. The voice was male and familiar. It was deep and almost menacing in tone. At first, she didn't recognize the voice, but the realization came in a wave of dread.

"Drakkius! What are you doing here?"

"The same as you, I presume. Visiting an old friend."

"I didn't know you two were close."

"Sarcasm? I thought after you ran away from Lux Enor in the royal carriage, you would have prepared a more civil tongue to speak to me. After all, I can still recall you to the capital."

"Forgive me, Lord Drakkius. I meant nothing by it, no sarcasm intended." She decided not to provoke him.

Drakkius stepped into the dim light, "I thought I told you to report to me in the throne room. I have heard nothing from you. What do you have to report?"

"The investigation of the Highlord's murder is still ongoing. I have a few leads but nothing definitive to report yet.

"Oh, what kind of leads?"

"There are rumors of unrest in the Sacred Land. I am there now to investigate any connection to the death of the Highlord. I used the portal in the White Tower to come here and consult the scribes. I thought maybe Morgoran might have seen something and me being so far away; I thought I would take advantage of the portals while I had the chance."

"Be two places at once, so to speak," Drakkius said.

"Yes, exactly. I knew the portals were intact."

Drakkius moved closer to her, "You would not lie to me, would you?"

"To what purpose?"

"It was naïve and reckless for you to leave Lux Enor the way you did. You could have stayed in the capital and investigated the crime scene more thoroughly." He walked over to Morgoran and examined the sleeping wizard. "Imagine my surprise to find you here, in the presence of your old mentor and master, when I thought you would be out there finding who killed our beloved Highlord."

He's toying with me. Shey thought. "I am here as part of the investigation. Morgoran could be very helpful."

"How?" Drakkius asked. He moved toward Shey increasing the volume of his voice with every step. "He can't even hold a thought in his head. He only sees the possible futures and after years and years of scribing only a handful of what he has spewed forth has been remotely accurate. What secret do you possess that no one has ever possessed for centuries that will allow you to interpret or understand anything he says?"

"I have none," Shey answered.

"You have none? Then, I will ask you again." His voice was sounding much calmer. "Why, are you here?"

Shey showed her disdain in her expression, "I asked you why you were here, not the other way around, and furthermore Morgoran is like a father to me. I don't need an ulterior motive to take the opportunity to see him when it presents itself." Shey noticed Morgoran stir. "You are waking Morgoran with your raised voice."

Drakkius stormed over to Morgoran and kicked his bed, "Then he will wake!"

Shey hurried to her mentor to check on him. "Stop it!"

"Sheyna Namear, you will return to your stolen royal coach and have the driver bring you back to Lux Enor immediately. You are on a fool's errand."

Shey felt for the stone in her pocket and then stealthily placed it in Morgoran's hand while Drakkius had his back turned and whispered. "I need you, Master."

Morgoran abruptly sat up in his bed, "Nightmares! Nightmares!" He yelled.

CHAPTER 10

VICIOUS

Morgoran stared at Drakkius for a moment; then his gaze became fixed on Shey. His clear eyes were voids in the middle of a canvas of white. He shook his head and blinked hard. When his eyes once again because fixed upon Shey, they returned to their glorious blue.

He backed away tossing his bedclothes to the side. "What in the god's names is happening? Where am I? Sheyna?"

"Morgoran, you have returned to us," Drakkius said. He reached out to the old wizard.

Morgoran jerked back, "Don't touch me! Don't you set one finger on me."

Drakkius feigned confusion. "Forgive me, Morgoran. I meant no offense."

"You will address me as Master, or have you forgotten I am one of the First Trine?"

"Forgive me...Master." Drakkius said with a bow.

"Master?" Shey queried.

"He is a disciple of Toborne, which makes him one of mine."

Drakkius coughed and then mustered a sheepish grin at Shey. "Toborne? One of the First Trine? I am not his disciple."

Morgoran scoffed, "You are. I have seen it. I do remember some of the visions I have had throughout this curse." He looked down at the stone in his hand. "Where did this come from?"

"I put it in your hand, Master," Shey admitted.

"A Lora Orbius. Well, you had better get to it then and ask me what you need answers to quickly. This thing will only negate the curse temporarily."

"Where did you get a dragon eye?" Drakkius said. He moved to look at the stone and Morgoran closed his fist around it.

"Never mind that. Master, do you know what is happening to the Sacred Land?"

"Aye, but is that really what you want to talk about?" He cut his eyes toward Drakkius.

"Oh, this is ridiculous; I am not going to dance around this. I am sure he already knows. He has been toying with me since I got here."

Drakkius closed his mouth, and his jaw clenched. His disdain was very apparent.

"The Sacred Land," Shey continued, "How long do we have?"

"It's difficult for me to say. I have been out of time for too long. I have no idea how much time has passed."

Drakkius replaced his disdain with satisfaction.

"What is it, Drakkius?" Shey asked. "Why are you so smug?"

"You will not find your answers here; that's why."

Morgoran stood up from the bed, "Quickly, listen to me, my apprentice and I will help you. There is one among you. This one can cause you much harm, but there is a blade that can help you. It's called Malinfel, and you can find it in the Jagged Mountains near the one who lies." He winked at her and then dropped the stone.

"Wait. What?" Shey stammered.

Morgoran sat back on his bed, the middle of his eyeballs began to swirl and finally returned to their clear state. He stood up and grabbed Drakkius by the shoulders, "Don't go to Brightonhold unless you want to taste defeat." He turned to Shey, "My apprentice, the fool returns. He is on his way here now." He gazed off into space as he relaxed back onto his bed. Shey put his bedclothes back and tucked him in again. When she was done, Drakkius looked her in the eye.

"So, you knew more than you let on earlier. You know about the Highlord, don't you."

"That you had him murdered? Yes, of course, I know. What did you expect?"

"I thought you might, but you held yourself so well I couldn't tell for sure until you brought Morgoran back." He reached down and picked up the Lora Orbius. "It's unfortunate this only has a one-time use. You wasted it. Such a shame."

"I wouldn't say that."

"Do you actually believe a magical blade will help you somehow? How gullible are you?"

"Morgoran would not lead me astray."

He tucked the stone into his pocket, "You know I can't let you go now. I was going to force you to return to Lux Enor where I would have you taken care of discretely. Now, I am afraid I will have to do it here all messy and inconvenient."

Shey began to draw in essence to fuel her magic.

"I can sense your essence, foolish. You are hardly a match for me."

Shey felt his essence too. It was very subtle and almost elegant. He had a refined approach that rivaled what she had felt from the Ianthill and Morgoran, members of the First Trine.

Shey decided she had to strike first before he could fully supply himself. She thought of her target, and she thought of fire. She released the essence, and a great fireball cascaded toward Drakkius. He dodged it and made it dissipate almost immediately.

"A bold choice in such close quarters. Are you trying to burn down the tower, kill Morgoran and all the sleeping scribes in the next room as well?"

"No," Shey said abruptly.

His swirled his right arm in a quick flourish, and Shey felt as though she had been struck in the stomach with a battering ram. She flew backward from the impact and into the wall. The blow had knocked all the breath out of her, and she failed to stand up fast enough before the second blow sent her against the wall again.

"You see, you are weak." He raised his hands to chest level ready to cast another. But before he let the essence flow through him, he stopped for a moment. Shey could hear what stayed his hand, a whistling noise coming from outside the open window. Drakkius took a step toward the window when he was pelted hard in the face by a flying silver flask.

Shey regained her footing and released her essence with a swirl of air trying to push Drakkius out the window. It was only partially successful with him grasping wildly at the window trim to stay inside. Shey bounded over to him kicking him in the backside as hard as she could. He gave way and fell from the window. Shey retrieved the flask and followed him to the grounds beyond. The drop from the window was only a few feet, and Drakkius was able to recover from his fall quickly, but Gondrial was there with his fist. He punched the man in his already bloodied nose, and the man fell backward.

"Gondrial! It's about time. I thought for a moment that Morgoran was wrong about the fool showing up."

"I'm not sure I know what you're talking about or that I like being called a fool, but I did sense your familiar essence signature, and when I felt his, I knew there was a fight on."

Drakkius got up and wiped the blood from his nose. Shey and Gondrial took a defensive stance. Drakkius began to smile and then laugh, "You think you have evened the odds?"

"Two against one is equal?" Gondrial asked. "What an arrogant jerk!"

Drakkius spit out some more blood from a bloodied lip. "You really are a fool."

Gondrial and Shey heard the unholy screech at that moment. It was coming from the skies above. Something big and winged coming from the dark of the skies. Then another screech from somewhere behind them.

Drakkius took a stone from his pocket. At first, Shey thought it was the Lora Orbius, but she soon realized it was a Lora Daine, a stone Dragon Knights used to travel instantaneously.

"Enjoy your gruesome deaths!" Drakkius said as he used the power of the dragon stone and was gone.

"I assume you have your daggers?" Gondrial asked.

"Always!"

Gondrial went his horse tied to a tree nearby and retrieved his sword. He untied his horse and slapped it on the rump to get it to bound away to safety. He unsheathed his sword and discarded the scabbard nearby; he swung his blade back and forth to warm up. Shey felt the familiar surge of essence in the air, and she took a cue from him and began to draw in her own. It was a tricky thing, essence, draw too much and it's like taking too much hot soup into your mouth, not only will it burn you before you can swallow, but you can't swallow it all at once either.

Gondrial hunkered down in an attack stance, bouncing slightly on his bent knees. Shey readied her daggers. The first monster swooped down onto the green grass spitting acid directly at Gondrial. He moved as quick as a cat from a striking serpent and the acid missed him, hissing as it contacted the grass behind him. Gondrial attacked the wings of the creature first, slicing the fleshy membranelike inner wing on the right side of the creature. It howled at him as he passed and pounced on him when he followed through with his attack.

Shey heard the sickly cry of the next creature come from behind. Her daggers became one with her hands and arms as she reacted, twisting her torso with eerie precision. Her duel daggers struck the thing in the chest, but one of her daggers bounced off the exoskeletal chest armor as her other dagger found flesh. It lurched causing her to lose her grip on the dagger still stuck in the creature's chest, and she fell to the side still clutching her right-handed blade. When she came to rest, she turned as quick as a whip to command her dagger still in the creature. She released some of the essence she had ready and made the dagger go in deeper and then slice upward through the thing's chest. It howled in pain and anger as it grabbed for the moving dagger. When it was about to grasp the dagger's handle, Shey made a yanking motion with her hand, and the dagger flew out the creature's chest and into her grip.

"Step aside!" Gondrial said as he rammed his sword down with both hands into Shey's' creature's chest. He pulled his blade, and in one swift motion, he severed the creature's head.

"The other one!" Shey shouted to him, "Where is the other one?" She knew he was trying to help her by neglecting his own fight. "You idiot, I am perfectly capable of..." The second creature came down on her from behind, acid spraying onto her arm and leg. She flipped it over her head, and it landed near Gondrial. She threw her daggers at it precisely cutting off its left arm before it swung down to bite Gondrial with its acidic maw. Its sharp teeth penetrated Gondrial's shoulder, and he cried out in pain. It tried to spread its wings and take off but the wing Gondrial had injured would not allow it. Shey commanded her daggers to finish it off. They sliced through it like it was hot butter and then returned to Shey. The acid on her arm and legs burned, and she used her dagger to cut away the section of her leather pants still burning with the acid. She glanced up at the sound of a blood-curdling screech to see a third creature a yard-lengths away. It sneered at them and then took to flight.

"Get that creature!" Shey shouted, but Gondrial was too busy trying to get his shirt off and stop the acid bite from spreading.

"Just let it go. We need to get into the Tower to the clerics. This acid is vicious."

"What the ogre's bum is going on here? What's all that commotion?" Shey recognized it was Kerad, the cleric of the Tower of Morgoran.

"Kerad! It's the Drasmyd Duil acid. We are both covered in it." Shey said.

Kerad rushed to her side and held the light of the lantern to see her better, "Lady Shey?" He moved the lantern up and down her body. "You are hardly *covered* in it."

"A little is enough!"

Others from the tower began to filter outside, "Here, you men take Lady Shey into my study." Kerad commanded, and several men went to her aid. Shey looked back as the hardiest of the men carried her lengthwise in his arms to see Kerad working on Gondrial's shoulder before the acidic bite went too deep. Men surrounded them both, and Shey knew he would be taken care of now. She turned back to her searing pain.

CHAPTER 11

ONE AMONG US

L ady Shey winced as she got up out of bed. Kerad, the cleric, rushed into her room, "My lady, I must protest. You need another day or two to recover."

"You let Gondrial go."

"He was very insistent."

"So am I. I must get back to Sylvalora and my coachman. They are waiting for me, and I am sure they are worried sick. I was supposed to return in a few hours, not a few days."

"I can't talk you out of traveling?"

"No, I am afraid not."

"Very well, but you realize I will have to report this to Morgoran."

Shey gave him an annoyed expression, "And you think he will comprehend what you are telling him?"

"He understands and remembers more than you might realize."

"I'll take my chances. Plus, it's been a long while since I was his apprentice. Morgoran himself couldn't stop me from returning to my obligations." With that Shey exited the room and quickly made her way to the portal. This time she could use essence to activate the portal rather than dragon magic. Her side had splitting pain, and she thought a moment about asking Kerad for some pain remedy, but she decided to travel instead. She was already tired of his healing lecture. She activated the portal and stepped through it. To her amazement, when she came through the other side in the White Tower, her pain was all but gone. Sylvalora was curled up in a newly cleaned corner with a blanket. She stirred awake when the portal dissipated with a loud hum.

"Shey, thank the gods. I was about to come after you."

"I was delayed because I was injured in a fight with two Drasmyd Duil at the Tower of Morgoran." She turned and twisted at the waist but still almost no pain. She let one side of her dress fall to examine the wound, and it was just a large bruise now. "I am healed; how?"

"It's the portal. It has built-in healing properties. Migarath thought it would be useful, but it ended up getting most of the portals destroyed during the War of the Oracle."

"I always thought they were destroyed so the enemy couldn't use them to escape."

"That too but imagine if you had one nearby where you could filter soldiers and wielders back and forth through."

"I see your point."

"There are more viable portals still around than people realize. One of Migarath's apprentices, who helped him develop the portals, managed to repair, or rebuild several of them after the war and before his untimely death."

"Why are they mostly forgotten then. It seems like they are something we need to keep around."

"Their construction is completely forgotten for one. When one breaks or stops working no one remembers how to fix it. Also, several of them are in places where magic has become outlawed, and then there are the few in Ishrak where no one would dare use them. But enough about the portals, did you see Morgoran and give him the Lora Orbius? How did you come to fight Drasmyd Duil?"

"Aye, I saw him, and yes, I gave him the stone. The curse was broken, but Drakkius was also there. The bastard summoned the Drasmyd Duil before he used a Lora Daine and disappeared."

"What did Morgoran say?"

"During his brief moment of lucidity, he said something about one among us who could create much harm, and he gave me a cryptic location of a sword that can help us."

"What sword?"

"Malfel or something like that."

"Malinfel?"

"Yes, that's the one. Morgoran said it was in the Jagged Mountains near the one who lies."

"I believe that Malinfel is a mindwielder sword. It was lost when the mindwielders were all but wiped out in the war. How are we supposed to use it?"

"It doesn't matter since I don't understand the clue to find it unless you do?"

"Yes, I do. It's near Soldier's Bluff. The one who lies is the soldier the village was named after."

"I thought it was named after a cliff or a bluff nearby."

Sylvalora chuckled. No, it was named after a soldier who won most of the town by bluffing his way in games of Nine Cards. When we exit into the white tower, I think we should keep all of this sword business to ourselves since Morgoran warned us about a possible betrayer."

"Agreed. Who could it be, Lyrrath? Geron? Rodraq?"

"Well, you brought Rodraq from Lux Enor. He could have been a spy planted to spy on you."

Shey sighed, "I don't know Lyrrath all that well either and he was acting strange the day I left for the Tower of Morgoran."

"What about Geron?"

"Geron? He's just a boy." Shey said. "And he's been through so much with losing his brother and parents. I can't believe he could be the one to betray us."

"Keep an eye out. We don't want to be surprised." Sylvalora said.

Shey nodded, "Come, let us join the others and get ready to travel out of here. After being in the Vale of Morgoran and able to feel essence again, I want to leave the barrenness of the Sacred Land as soon as we possibly can."

When Shey and Sylvalora returned to the common room of the white tower, Geron was drawing on a piece of parchment with a piece of charcoal and Rodraq was staring out the window.

"Rodraq, get the team hitched and ready the coach," Shey commanded.

"Thank the gods!" Rodraq said. "I am about to go out of my head! Where are we going?"

"Back East, toward the Jagged Mountains."

"Good deal!" Rodraq said heading with haste toward the door.

"Where's Lyrrath?" Sylvalora asked him before he left.

"He's wandering around outside. He's probably as stir-crazy as I am." With that, he exited.

"Geron, dear, gather yourself. We are moving out as soon as Rodraq brings the coach." The boy nodded and went to the wash basin to clean his dirty hands. Shey went over to the drawing out of curiosity. "Geron! What is this?" The drawing looked like a Drasmyd Duil coming out of shadows. It was almost a professional drawing like the ones she had seen artists at the court in Lux Enor draw.

"I don't know. It's just a monster I made up."

Shey held up the parchment so Sylvalora could see it. She was concerned when she took a corner of the picture in her hand.

"Geron, have you seen a creature like this before?"

He was busy drying his hands, "No, wait, yes! I think one hurt the men at the Defender Patrol cabin." He began to whimper.

"Oh, come here," Shey said. He ran to her, and she took him up in her arms.

Sylvalora patted the boy on the back. "it's all right boy. We will keep you safe from them."

Shey pushed the boy back, "Be strong now and help me gather up some provisions for the trip."

The boy smiled, and Shey chose to believe the odd smirk was the boy's joy at traveling with them again.

Rodraq had the coach out in front of the White Tower a few moments after Shey, Geron, and Sylvalora finished gathering up foodstuffs. He took the packs and wrapped goodies and stored them in the truck he strapped to the rear of the vehicle among other storage areas of the opulent coach. Shey watched him all the while feeling a pang of regret for taking such a lavish wagon. It was sure to stick out as they traveled through the small towns and villages. When she took the coach, she wanted it to be seen and feared but now that she knew the truth the coach was unsuitable.

"Rodraq, can we do something about this coach?"

"Sure, what do you want to do to it?"

"I want to make it look more...common."

Rodraq laughed, "How do you expect to do that, by magic?"

"I could!" Shey said sarcastically.

"I don't think the high council of Lux Enor would appreciate that."

"I could change it back afterward."

He clamped his mouth shut.

"I'm joking. Magic of the kind it would take to transmogrify this coach is specialized. My magic would be like taking a hammer to a silver teapot. I could transform it, but no one would be able to ride in the blasted thing."

"Oh, well. I could stop in one of the villages along the way and borrow another coach. A more common coach."

"You could do that?"

"I know a few people. It can be done."

"All right. Switch them out whenever you get the chance."

"Aye," he said.

Lyrrath pulled himself up onto the driver's seat, "I think I will travel up here, my lady."

"Whatever suits you, Lyrrath." She answered with a weak smile before Rodraq helped her step into the coach.

Inside the coach Shey watched Geron get comfortable in the seat across from hers. Sylvalora was in the seat next to her fixated on something outside the window. Shey took a deep breath and laid her hands in her lap. She decided it would be best if she didn't voice her fear that Lyrrath might be the one to betray them in front of Geron.

It was after a day's worth of traveling and an uncomfortable stay near a rocky outcropping near the border of the Sacred Land when Shey instructed Rodraq to pick up the pace to a point where the houses would not be too taxed, but at least they would be moving faster than they had been traveling. She breathed a sigh of relief when they were close enough to the border of the Sacred Land that she could feel the touch of essence again.

"We need to find Geron a new home." She whispered to Sylvalora while Geron slept.

"We should have done that long ago."

"I know, but he is supposed to be a seer, and I wanted to see if there was any truth to it."

Sylvalora watched the sleeping boy. "Maybe it was his brother. I haven't seen anything from him that indicates any kind of special ability."

"No! don't leave me somewhere!" Geron said rubbing the sleep from his eyes. "I want to stay with you."

"We will keep you with us until we find a suitable place for you, don't worry," Sylvalora said.

"No! forever."

"Nothing is forever," Shey said.

The boy's eyes rolled in the back of his head, and he began to sway his head back and forth. "Lady Shey, an old friend will come and betray you."

Shey gave Sylvalora a knowing glance before she turned back to the boy, "It's okay, Geron. You don't have to pretend to be a seer."

Geron straightened up, "But I can see."

"We will explore that road when and if we come to it. For now, don't worry about it." Shey reached to him and put her hand on his knee to reassure him. "I promise we will not leave you somewhere without your wanting to stay there on your own, okay?"

Geron nodded.

"Now, when we get to Soldier's Bluff, I want you to do as we tell you, exactly as we tell you. It might be dangerous. Then, after we leave the village, we will be heading to Brookhaven under disguises. Can you remember all that?"

Geron nodded.

"Good. Now, I don't want you to fret about us leaving you anywhere. We will all talk about it before we do anything."

"I wasn't kidding before. The betrayer is Lyrrath. I have seen it." Geron said.

"Now, Geron. I told you there is no need to prove yourself." Shey said.

"He's not who you believe he is anymore. You have already noticed he is acting strange, especially to me because I know of his true intentions."

"Be that as it may, we need to discuss this another time. We are nearing Soldier's Bluff."

"All right," Geron said as he laid his head down again and closed his eyes.

Shey gave Sylvalora a worried look right before she thought she saw Geron smiling for a moment.

CHAPTER 12

GONDRIAL'S RUN

A few hours before nightfall Gondrial arrived in Cedar Falls. He made his way to The Eagle and the Hare Inn where he stabled his horse and reserved a room for the night. After putting away his personal belongings, he went to the common room for an ale and a meal. He was not particularly worried about the Enforcers at this point. He had left them stumbling over themselves several leagues back. He had been toying with them by projecting his essence back and forth through the woods and once down into the bottom of a ravine. The two were probably still down there searching in vain for a magic wielder they would never find. The prospect put a smile on his face.

"Who are ye grinning at?" Gondrial suddenly realized he was face to face with a burly fellow dressed in the sturdy brown material of the mountain folk, and the man was mistaking his amused grin for a challenge.

"Oh, nothing. I was just in thought. I wasn't looking at anyone in particular."

"I thought ye were grinning at me."

"No, friend. I was just grinning."

The man plopped down in the chair at the table next to him and leaned back to speak, "Where did you get them fancy clothes?"

Gondrial looked down at his black leather and cloth ensemble, "In Symbor, I believe." He tried to be as bland as he could in hopes the man would get the hint; he had no interest in speaking with him any further.

"Hey, you talk purdy."

Now, Gondrial felt a bit annoyed, "I'm busy, could I please ignore you some other time?"

"What did you just say to me?" The burly man was stunned.

"Look, I'm sure you're just trying to be friendly, but I have been on the road all day, and I just want to be left in peace. I hope you don't mind."

"I don't understand."

Gondrial briefly looked at the man before turning back to his mug of ale, "Well, I'm only responsible for what I say, not for what you understand."

The man turned away when the inn maiden asked him what he wanted to order from the kitchen. A few moments later another two men of the mountain folk, by the looks of them, joined the burly man. Gondrial had no choice to be to listen. None of them seemed to have any control over the volume of their voices.

"Tell him about the bird man." The first of the men to sit down began.

"Oh, I don't think it was a bird man. It was more like a flying lizard." Said the second man.

This immediately got Gondrial's attention.

"What are ye fools talking about now?" The burly man asked.

"Tell him, Sven."

Gondrial turned to face the blond mountain man named Sven.

"We were ridin' to town, and I saw this dark-cloaked man hunched over something in the field next to a bunch of trees. At first, I didn't think much about it but as I watched it turned to me, and the hair stood up on the back of me neck! The thing had red eyes and a gaping maw; blood was trickling down from its sharp teeth. I looked a little closer, and I saw the green cloak of a traveler."

"Aye," the second man said, "Sven thought it might be eatin' someone from the road."

"Well, we saw that and picked up the pace from there. I tried not to look back but my fear got the best of me, and I turned to look at the road, and the thing was few paces behind us on the road but was facing away from us. It stretched out its wings, let out a screech, and climbed into the air." Sven said.

"Which way was it flying?" Gondrial asked.

"Excuse me?"

"Sorry, I think I might have seen it too," Gondrial said.

"Oh, it was flying back toward the mountains."

"I'll be damned; the stupid thing turned back." He clenched his fists in frustration, "It doubled back!"

"You saw it too?" The unnamed man asked.

"Yes, all too close. It's heading back for Shey." The men looked confused. Gondrial tossed a coin onto their table, "Here, have a round of drinks on me."

"Hey, I know ye were a good fella." The burly man said, but Gondrial could only think about getting back to Shey. He smiled at the men and put down more coin for his meal and drink. He was heading for the door when the two Enforcers he had been running from, entered. He quickly ducked back toward the bar. "Damn it!" He muttered.

The arrival of the Enforcers quieted the room. They looked around for a moment and then went to sit at a nearby table. It wasn't long before Gondrial felt the familiar swell of someone gathering essence. At first, he thought he might have been drawing it himself, but he quickly realized it wasn't coming from him. He looked at the Enforcers. They both had stunned expressions and were looking right at him. He felt the essence from behind, and he turned to see the bar maiden frozen in fear. She was only a step or two away from him.

"Stop it!" He whispered urgently. You are drawing in magic. They can sense you do it!"

"I can't help it. I do it when I get nervous."

"Control it!"

"I can't."

Gondrial peered at the Enforcers. They were getting up and still looking in his direction. Gondrial sighed, "Stay behind me. They are coming over here for you."

"Everyone stay where you are." The first Enforcer said. "We are here on Enforcer business. Stay out of our way, and no one will get hurt."

"No one try to be the hero here." The second one said, "This will be over, and we will get out of your inn peacefully. "

"Well, that's not going to work for me," Gondrial said. "In fact, I have a real problem with it."

"Sir, stay where you are." The first Enforcer stated.

"You don't recognize me?" Gondrial asked.

They examined his face, "No, should we?"

Gondrial grinned, "Thick as you can be, I see."

"Sir!"

"I have been running from you for a while. You tried to catch me in Seabrey a time back. You guys are so easy to evade. It's embarrassing."

The pair looked at each other perplexed then they moved forward, "Step aside, fool. We need to take the girl."

Gondrial scratched his head nonchalantly, "You see. I can't let you do that." He stood defiant.

"No, sit down, friend." Sven pleaded. "You don't want to get mixed up with their sort."

"Aye, friend. Sit back down." The Enforcer said.

Gondrial tossed the wooden chair he had been sitting on into the air, and it froze in place. Ribbons of purple and gold sparkles began to play around it, and the chair broke into several pieces, which hung ominously in the air pointed close to the Enforcer's heads. He winked at Sven, "Wizard battle. I suggest you run." Sven got up from the table knocking over his chair quickly followed by his friends. "Wait!" Gondrial motioned with his head, "Take the girl to safety, and keep in mind that if you fail, I will hunt you down."

The burly man nodded and took the girl by the arm to lead her toward the back.

"Wait, come back here." One of the Enforcers commanded.

"Go! Like I said." Gondrial let the essence ribbons flow around the pieces of the chair keeping the Enforcers at bay. "You will not take her."

"You give yourself away to protect a novice?"

"Aye, why do you want her so badly? I am here obviously not a novice, but you are interested in her?"

"What is it to you? She is no one to you." The first Enforcer said.

"I just think men like you should go after wizards your own size." He felt the Enforcers drawing in essence. "Hey, I don't suppose you both will just forget about all this and leave the way you came?"

The first Enforcer shook his head, "I am afraid not. You say you're a wielder we have been following?"

"Did I say that?"

"I don't remember chasing you in Seabrey." The second said.

"I thought you saw...oh, I see. You didn't get a good look at me. I haven't used any essence up until now and no offense, but you both seemed pretty dumb?"

"Go ahead and keep insulting us. It just makes this easier. Surrender yourself. Let the chair fall and dissipate your essence ribbons."

"Nope, can't do that. I have somewhere I need to be."

Gondrial didn't see the Enforcer sympathizer behind him with the bottle until it was too late. The glass shattered in a streak of pain across the top of his head. There was some liquid flowing down his face, and some dizziness, a thought or two about it being a shame someone was wasting good corn mash, and then the chair crashed to the floor. He got a brief look at his assailant on his way down just before everything went dark. It was the burly man.

Gondrial awoke with a crushing headache. He tried to draw in essence even though it was even more painful on his already throbbing head, none came. He looked at his wrists and clicked the irons around them. They were Enforcer irons, essence suppressors. He couldn't draw in enough to cast. *I wish I had Shey's dragon magic at times like these.* He thought. Once his head cleared a little more, he thought of the girl and what that scoundrel might have done to her. Well, he warned the man. If anything happened to the girl, he would hunt them down, and he meant it! He forced himself up. He was in a wooden cell with stale straw strewn about the floor. There were bars on the window and flat iron bars on the cell door. He examined the iron squares to see how well the cross irons were affixed to the vertical bars. A few were weak.

"Well, it's a good thing I have had a lot to drink." He said before removing his tunic to take off his soft cloth undershirt. "Stupid Enforcers, this isn't my first jail." He put the shirt on the floor and began to urinate on it. Once it was soaked, he wrapped it around the bars and began twisting it. The flexible cloth pulled the bars together breaking the studs holding the crossbars to the vertical. "By the gods, I swear I will take that burly fellow's head off for making me have to do this!" He said as liquid ran down his arms. He moved the shirt to the next square and then the next until he had broken most of the bars apart far enough to crawl through them. He sneaked to the front area of the cells. The village was small enough that there was no guard on duty. He did notice brazier and stove were lit; a pot of bittering tea was set on it to boil. "Ah, they just stepped out for a moment," He said. He took the shirt and laid it across the top of the pot letting the edges of it fall on the hot surface.

"There, a small token of my contempt for jail cells." He said as the stench from the steam coming from the shirt had begun to fill the room. Gondrial slipped out the door and to the back of the building. He stopped briefly to put his tunic back on and then headed for the nearest blacksmith. As it happened, he knew the blacksmith's apprentice, a big, young man with no love for the Enforcers or the warden. His friend would be able to remove the Enforcer's shackles, and as soon as Gondrial was free, he would track the girl. He hoped the betraying scoundrel would still be around when he caught up to her.

CHAPTER 13

LURKER IN THE SHADOWS

Gondrial left the blacksmith's shop with a new undershirt, sore wrists, and three gold pieces lighter in the purse. He was determined to take that gold out of the burly man's hide if he was still with the girl. He didn't wait around long enough for the Enforcers to look for him. He knew the blacksmith shop would probably be one of the first places they would look for him, so he hung the broken shackles on a hook near the front entrance. It served Henrick right for charging him three gold! He traipsed sufficiently into the nearby woods before he attempted to gingerly draw the essence need to see where the girl had gone. If he were subtle enough, the Enforcers would be unable to detect him from the natural vibrations of the essence of all things. It was when folks tried to draw in large amounts that the Enforcers were alerted. He concentrated in order not to draw in too much, and then he released the essence with the words *find her*. Essence magic could be a tricky thing but at low levels, but he was pleasantly surprised when he saw a slightly luminous trail snake out before him.

Thick rainclouds blew in from the west as Gondrial moved stealthily through the twisting back streets of Cedar Falls. Not only would the Enforcers be looking for him soon for escaping their capture, but now he had to hurry to stay ahead of the deluge of rain that was sure to come when the clouds unleashed their heavy burden. The essence trail led him outside of town toward the east, the exact direction he wanted to go. Once he knew if the girl was safe, he would rush east to pursue the creature flying toward Lady Shey. But, of the two, he thought Shey and Sylvalora stood the better chance of fighting off the Drasmyd Duil than the girl did fighting off the Enforcers and the burly man. He wasn't far out of town when he spotted the Enforcers returning to Cedar Falls. Gondrial let the essence trail drop as they neared. He found a spot in the brush where he would be difficult to spot, and he laid low as the two men passed.

"It has been a most productive day." The first Enforcer was saying.

"Indeed, we got the girl and the idiot who thought he could protect her."

"It was a capital idea to separate the two. The fool in the cells would have done something rash if he thought the girl was close by."

You are not wrong, Gondrial mused to himself.

"Come, those skies are looking like rain, and we have a brisk walk still ahead." The first Enforcer said as they picked up the pace.

Gondrial waited for them to get sufficiently down the road before he left his hiding place and headed up the road. He speculated from the Enforcer's conversation that the girl must be in the custody of the burly man, and perhaps his friends, ahead somewhere. He let his essence trail return, and it snaked out in front of him again, this time a bit stronger than before. They were not far down the road. He doubled back and made his way back to town, careful not to run into the Enforcers or the town's warden. At the Eagle and the Hare, he retrieved his horse and saddle and paid the stablemaster, who told him about some commotion going on over at the warden's office. Gondrial smiled and acted surprised at the news.

The stablemaster gave him his change and stared at him for a moment as Gondrial mounted his horse, "Say, what are you in such a hurry for anyway?"

Gondrial reigned his horse, "I'm probably the trouble you're talking about." He smiled and tipped his finger to his forehead as he spurred the horse onward. If the stablemaster had anything to say Gondrial didn't hear it. He rode the backstreets to get out of town and then increased his pace once he was clear of prying eyes. He galloped down the road east. He hoped that the men who had the girl would be in no big hurry. In the back of his mind, he wondered what the Enforcers were doing to pursue him, which he was sure they would do, but he let the thought die. He had been in much worse situations, and he had always been able to get on with his life. Having a friend in high places, like Lady Shey, did have its advantages.

When Gondrial spotted the horse and rider up ahead, he was surprised that the burly man was the only Enforcer with the girl. Then, his elven sight detected movement in the tree line. Two others were traveling along with them.

Gondrial rode off to the side and got off his horse. "Horse," He said. "I'm not going to tie you up. Can you be ready for me if I whistle for you?"

The horse neighed as if it understood him.

"Good boy," Gondrial said patting the horse's nose. He left the horse and bounded along the trees on the opposite side of the road from where the other traveled. As he neared the horse and riders, he realized the guards on the side were crisscrossing the road ahead and behind, hiding in case someone like Gondrial were to try and sneak up on them. He wasn't sure how to approach the situation. All three men looked pretty tough, and surely at least one of them could detect essence if he tried to use magic. If only he could find a way to get a message to the girl. He was psyching himself up to jump at one of the flanking men when the burly man on the horse suddenly stopped.

"What's that up ahead gents?" The burly man pointed ahead.

Gondrial craned his neck trying to get a better look.

"It looks like an overturned wagon." One of the flanking men said.

"Be cautious; it's most likely a trap." The second flanking man said.

Gondrial stayed back and followed the men as they approached the accident. From what Gondrial could see, it was an overturned wagon. Personal effects were scattered out all around it, and the visible front wheel was broken in half.

"The front wheel is shattered." One of the men called back. "I think it made the thing overturn."

"Where are the horses?" The burly man said looking around. Gondrial ducked when he looked his way.

"No horses," the first man said. "They must have run off."

"Any people?"

The first man rummaged through the debris, "By the gods, aye, a boy here!"

Gondrial saw his opportunity. He could pretend he was the wagon driver. He prepared himself and then stepped out of the shadows just inside to hear the girl screaming. His eyes fell on the first Enforcer to see the man's face as it contorted under pain of his arm being ripped from its socket. The second man reacted swiftly and rushed to the first man's aid. A swooshing sound over Gondrial's head made him drive for cover in the brush. He spun and recovered in time to see several winged creatures, much smaller than the Drasmyd Duil, fly over toward the men.

"Dramyds!" The burly man shouted, "Look out!" But it was too late; the creatures attacked the man with vicious ferocity. The man with the girl spurred his horse and tried to ride off, but that just attracted the monsters. The horse lost its footing and fell. The burly man came back up with a sword in hand, and the girl rolled to the side, still handcuffed. Gondrial stepped out of his hiding place and let the essence flow through him. The man immediately turned to him when he felt the essence and his face melted from terror into relief, which Gondrial found ironic. The man began to swing at the nearby Dramyds with his sword slicing through some of them.

Lightning streaked across the sky, illuminating there were more of the creatures flying above than Gondrial had believed. He released the essence, and the lightning above responded to him by striking down on the Dramyds closer to the ground, electrocuting many of them with one well-placed strike. Small streaks of lightning danced over Gondrial's fingers. He raised his hands into the air and pointed at the Dramyds circling above as they entered into a dive toward him. He released his magic and lightning came from both his fingers and the skies above. Several monstrous bodies thudded as they fell to the ground in little black heaps. He rushed to the man, who was standing protectively with the girl at his back, "Attack them! You are in Enforcer; you have magic too."

"I...I can't. I have never used my magic like that."

"Stupid Enforcers, all you know is suppression, hypocrisy, and hate!" he sent another bolt of lightning to a charging Dramyd as the rain began to fall in sheets. "At least use that sword!" *I can't believe I was afraid to attack these cowards*, Gondrial thought.

The man nodded and moved forward. He lifted the blade as his head came off and rolled to Gondrial's feet. The original Drasmyd Duil stood where the man's body fell. It lurched at Gondrial next, but he evaded it and rolled next to the girl. He reached out quickly and picked up the burly man's big sword. Hold out your hands. The girl held out her chained hands out. He stood upright, The Drasmyd Duil charged again, and Gondrial sent another bolt of lightning at it, knocking it back. Stay very still. He released his magic through the sword, and he swung it over his head and then down, slicing through the chain in the middle of the shackles. Once the cuffs were separated, they both opened and fell away from her hands. She rubbed her wrists.

"Can you wield?"

"What?"

"Can you use magic."

"Some." She said.

"Good, get ready then!" He pointed up to the sky as a bolt of lightning exposed more of the creatures coming for them.

"Um, sir?"

"What is it?" Gondrial said moving toward the girl. There were now two of her.

"I think this one is trying to trick you." One girl said.

"No, she is." Said the other.

"We don't have time for this!" Gondrial said.

"I can give you the sight." One girl said. Gondrial felt something that felt like a worm crawling through his forehead. He almost dropped the sword. He closed his eyes, and when he opened them, one girl looked like herself, and the other was hideous, like a mixture of a Drasmyd Duil and the girl. He swung his sword and caught the creature by surprise. His blade severed its head. He nodded at the girl, "There's more coming."

"You can see them as I can now."

"That's useful. Wild magic?"

The girl nodded.

"Stay behind me," Gondrial commanded as the smaller Dramyds attacked.

Bolts of lightning streaked across the sky as Gondrial let loose his magic. Several more of the creatures fell, and then they began to fly erratically before leisurely flying off toward the northeast. "I think they lost their commander when I killed the Drasmyd Duil imitating you." He let the sword fall limply. The rain began to subside a little, and he saw for the first time that the girl had been injured at some point during the fight. He leaned down to her examining the wounds on her arm and cut into her side. "You're hurt."

"Aye," she said. "I think it was when we fell from the horse."

"What's your name?" Gondrial asked so he could distract her from what he was doing.

"Deylia." She said.

"Where are you from, Deylia?" He asked as he tightened a makeshift cloth bandage on her arm.

She winced, "I am from Trigothia. I came here on a merchant trip with my father, but I couldn't control my wild magic anymore once we were in Symboria and he was killed trying to protect me in Symbor from Enforcers."

"Aye, there is something about the Sacred Land in Symboria that brings out the wild magic. I have seen it happen before."

"The Enforcers in Trigothia can be bribed, and my father made the mistake of trying to bribe a couple here. They didn't like it."

"You are much closer to their main headquarters over here. The Enforcers aren't as corruptible. There, I should be able to transport you now."

"What about the others?"

Gondrial looked around at the carnage, "I am afraid we will have to leave them as they are."

"That's barbaric. You can't bury them?"

"Not if you want to live. You have been bitten by a Dramyd. I must get you to a cleric. There are a few in Brookhaven, or we can go to the Vale of Morgoran, but I have business to the east, toward Brookhaven so, that's the way we're going."

Deylia reluctantly agreed.

Gondrial stood up and whistled loudly. A few moments later his horse, named Horse, came galloping up. Gondrial helped Deylia mount up, and then he slipped on behind her. "Hold on, and I will get you some help."

Deylia nodded.

The rain began to fall again as they rode northeast on the Southern Road.

CHAPTER 14

THE SWORD

The winds had begun to blow out of the North when Shey's coach reached the Sea and Ale Inn, a funny name considering the nearest large body of water was a several day's ride to the south. It was close enough; however, to offer fresh fish and other seafood. Shey was looking forward to dining on something besides road rations for a change. She was even more excited to have fish instead of beef stock and stew.

Rodraq lowered the steps and opened the coach door. "We've arrived." He announced.

"Rodraq," Shey began as she stepped onto the first step. "Do you still believe you can switch the coach for a common wagon?"

Rodraq chuckled, "Aye, my lady."

"Rodraq?"

"Sorry, my lady, it's just that you sound like a proper royal."

"Yes, well, I had better work on that while we are here and before we travel on to Brookhaven under disguise."

"Aye, my lady."

Sylvalora and Geron followed with Geron rushing past Shey to get inside the inn. Shey turned to Sylvalora. "The boy says he's hungry."

"I should say so," Shey said.

"Go on, my lady. I will take care of the coach." Rodraq said.

Shey followed Geron into the inn and procured a couple of rooms for the night. Once the room business was concluded she sat with Geron and Sylvalora in the common room to order a bite to eat. A portly yet friendly young man made his way to the table. He was obviously very nervous, and Shey realized it was probably due to her manner of dress and her reputation. Everyone knew about the coach. It would be much better after Rodraq replaced it with another carriage.

"What may I bring you?" The young man asked.

"What do you have that's good?" she raised her finger before he could answer, "and I should mention I prefer fresh food."

"We have a wonderful fish stew. It was prepared fresh a few hours ago." He said before his friendly expression contorted into one of terror.

"You are wrinkling your nose, dear," Sylvalora said to her.

"Oh, am I. I am so sorry. It's just; I was thinking earlier that every inn I have visited lately seems only to serve stew."

"Oh," the man's expression returned to its friendly humor, "We do have the catch of the day. The cooks can have a filet prepared for you in no time."

"Aye, I will have the filet." She looked at Geron. "What do you want to eat?"

"Fish stew is fine for me."

"I'll have the same," Sylvalora said. "No need to go to any special trouble for us."

"I'll return shortly." The young man said before heading off for the kitchens.

"When did you become so spoiled, Shey?" Sylvalora asked as she unrolled a cloth napkin. "That court position you held has made you a snob."

"So you and Gondrial say, I just noticed the young man was already nervous and obviously already knew who I was, so I thought why pretend and choke down yet another bowl of stew."

"I don't believe it!" Sylvalora said.

"Well, I don't know why not. He was falling all over himself to get here."

"No, not that, look at what's above the fireplace affixed high on the mantel."

Shey turned in her chair to get a better look. The inn-sized fireplace had a wide stone façade, which was adorned with a net draped over a stuffed fish of some kind with a rusty harpoon sticking out of it. There were various seashells and starfish decorating the net. Just above the net, and somewhat out of place, was a soldier's helm with a rather plain looking, rusty sword hilt just visible above it. If the hilt had a blade to it, the thing was not visible due to it being buried under all the other adornments. "What? the fishnet and the harpoon or the helm and sword?"

"The sword. If my memory serves that hilt is the hilt of Malinfel."

"No," Shey squinted to get a better look, "That can't be the sword. What would it be doing here as a decoration? Look at it; it's rusty and cheap. It must be a copy, a bad copy."

A moment later the plump young man returned with a tray food. He plopped the food almost recklessly in front of them. Shey caulked his manner up to nerves.

"Say, I noticed there is a sword behind the fishnet on the mantel," Shey said.

The plump man squinted, "So there is. I never noticed it before."

"Never?"

"The net and harpoon have been there as long as I have worked here. I remember it here even when I used to come here with my mum when I was a lad."

"Where is the owner of the inn? Might they know?"

"I doubt it, but you might ask old Dane at the bar. He was also here when I was a boy. I think he has been here as long as the building has been standing. I bet he could tell you about the sword and what not."

"Thank you. I will have a word with him once I am done eating."

Sylvalora took a bite of her fish stew, "So, you do believe it might be the sword."

Shey was irritated, but she didn't want Sylvalora to see, "Well, it doesn't hurt to inquire does it. I still doubt the sword has been attached to a mantle at an inn for years. How did it get here and why would it be used as decoration?"

"Malinfel is forgotten magic. Maybe they didn't know what they had."

"It's not very forgotten if Morgoran thinks it might help us. He also told me about it in front of Drakkius."

"I meant in construction."

Shey set down her napkin, "Wait here and eat your stew. I will talk to the barman and see if I can get an answer to this quickly so I can have some peace."

"You're the one getting all riled up about it, dear," Sylvalora said.

Shey sighed, got up and weaved between the plain wooden tables to the bar at the west end of the common room. The mantle was located directly opposite on the east wall.

"Hello, my lady." The barman said when Shey approached. "What can I do for you?"

"I was told you have been employed here for quite some time. Is that true?"

"Near thirty years now, aye, my lady."

"Good, I wondered if you might tell me about the sword located under the net and harpoon on the mantle?"

"Certainly, what did you wish to know?"

"Where did it come from and why is it up there in the mantle? Is it just a decorative sword?"

"That sword came from a cave not far from here. When the owner of this place was a boy, his Pa built the place. I know because I was his best friend. We used to go explore the old caves and get into all sorts of mischief." His gaze drifted off.

"Uh hum, you were saying?"

"Oh yes, sorry. Say, has anyone ever told you, you have the most striking blue eyes?"

"Many, many times, now, you were saying?"

"Oh, sorry, I didn't mean to offend?"

"None taken. I am just very interested in the sword."

"Well, interested or not, you would have a better chance if you were to go to the smithy and have one made for you."

"Ah, so the smithy has reproduced the sword?"

"Oh sure, that is a most common arming sword design around here. It's nothing special."

"That's what I thought. Thank you, kind sir." Shey turned to go back to her table.

"Except for that one. It is a magical sword."

Shey stopped in mid-stride. She stepped back to the bar, "Why do you say that?"

"When we found the sword, Jeroh, that's the current owner, used to use it to cut wood and use it for other such general abuse until the blade was dulled. It sat around collecting dust until the original inn was renamed the Soldier and the Sword. After that, the sword was placed upon the mantle with the helm."

"Okay, and you think it's magic because...?"

"The Inn burned down. Everything but the mantle was lost. When the inn was rebuilt, it was named the Sea and Ale, and they tried to take down the sword and helm to put up the net and harpoon, only the sword and helm would not budge. Presumably, the helm had been fused by the fire to the mantle. They tried everything, but short of destroying the mantle, they couldn't remove it."

"The sword was fused too?"

"No, that's the magic part. The heat didn't do anything to it visibly like it did the helm. But they still could not remove it. There was no reason for it to cling to that wall, but it would not budge. Eventually, they just put up the Sea and Ale decorations over it."

"Thank you for the story," Shey said.

"You don't believe me, do you."

"Of course, I do. It's just not the sword I'm looking for."

"It talks to people." He said.

"It what?"

"The sword talks to people. It dares them to try and remove it, but the owner won't let anyone try. A couple have even tried without permission and got thrown out of here for their trouble."

"Is that why you believe it to be magic?"

The old barman nodded.

Shey did her best to give the old-timer a genuine smile, "Thank you so much for your story. I enjoyed talking with you."

"Any time. I always have time to talk with a pretty woman."

"Aw, you're so sweet." She said waving her hand at him dismissively.

He beamed back at her and then began to absently run a semi-white rag across the bar as he had undoubtedly done thousands of times.

Shey weaved back through the tables to Sylvalora and Geron.

"Well?" Sylvalora asked.

"It's just a normal arming sword, reproduced many times over by the local smithy."

"Disappointing."

"Surely, you didn't think Malinfel would be that easy to find?"

Sylvalora laughed and then looked at the sword hilt sticking out from under the fishing net, "Finding a magical sword hanging haphazardly on the mantle of an inn. In the common room no less."

"Ridiculous!" Shey agreed.

"Apparently, some boys twenty some odd years ago stumbled across that sword in a cave nearby."

"I wonder who would leave their arming sword in a cave?" Sylvalora asked.

"Someone probably hid it there expecting to return to retrieve it when they needed it."

"That seems a bit odd."

"Of course, maybe since the sword pattern is so common, it was just left there and forgotten. I mean, why does there have to have a reason? I'm sure it isn't all that strange for a couple of young explorers to find odds and ends lying about. People find things in strange places all the time."

"That's true. I once found some old scrolls in a cave; they were sealed in clay jars. No one knows who left them there."

"Oh, were they important?"

"Ianthill took them to study, and he never got back to me, so I think not."

"A pity."

Shey gazed up at the rusty sword hilt again. "Did you know the barman told me they used to chop at wood with that sword? They dulled the blade playing with it."

Sylvalora chuckled, "You're kidding?"

"No, they did."

"It's a good thing; it's just a common everyday arming sword with no significance."

"Aye, a proper sword should be treated with respect."

Sylvalora let her coy laughter trail off, "So, how are we going to get it down?"

Shey took a bite of her now room temperature fish, "In the middle of the night when no one is watching, of course."

"Then we will rush off to Brookhaven?"

"Precisely, disguised, just as we have discussed," Shey said.

CHAPTER 15

THE INN AT THE EDGE

G ondrial and Deylia reached the mountain village of Brookhaven just before dark on the second day from Cedar Falls. Deylia, injured by the poisonous saliva of a Dramyd, was in good spirits but the poison was beginning to take its toll on her. Gondrial slowed the damage with an herbal remedy he learned along with a small, undetectable amount of magic. It was enough to keep her alive until they reached the Temple of Loracia in Brookhaven. He galloped through the streets past the Tiger's Head Inn and its wonderful smells of roasting meat and soothing pinewood fires. He came to a stop in front of the Temple.

"Aid, Aid here!" He shouted as he dismounted and began to help Deylia down from his horse. A teenager with blond hair and a pleasant face, wearing the white robes of a priest of Loracia exited the temple to help Gondrial get the girl inside.

"What happened?" The blond young man asked.

"Dramyd attack," Gondrial said.

The boy was confused, "What's a Dramyd?"

"Never mind. Where is Father Tarle?"

"I'm here." A man with an even more elaborate white and gold robe came in from a room behind the altar. He was older with white hair and a short white beard. He appeared exceptionally clean as if he had never had a spec of dirt touch him in his entire life. "What happened?"

"Dramyd bite," Gondrial explained.

"Ah," He turned to the young man, "Vesperin, get some clean linen and some drinking water. Bring them to the healing room and then go to Sanmir and ask him for some of his yellow salve; he will know what I am talking about."

"Yes, Father," Vesperin said and hurried off.

"Where in Loracia's name did you come across a Dramyd?" Father Tarle asked.

"Dramyds, there were a lot of them."

The priest pursed his lips as if he didn't believe Gondrial, "Help me get her to the healing room."

"Aye, and I can see you don't believe me, but the girl can attest I am telling you the truth."

The priest shook his head, "It isn't my place to question. I am merely here to heal. I will take care of her. Once we get her to the healing room, you can go. Return in a couple of hours, and I will give you her condition."

"I promised her I would stay with her."

"Nonsense, go and get out of my way, now. I don't need you underfoot. I am sure the girl would understand." He said caustically.

"I thought priests of Loracia were supposed to be nice old men and women," Gondrial said.

"That was me being nice!" Tarle said.

"Oh."

Gondrial helped get Deylia to the healing room. She was unconscious now, and Tarle shooed him out of the room as soon as he could. The priest was joined by two more women and the boy Vesperin as Gondrial was almost pushed physically out of the healing room.

Gondrial left the temple and headed directly for the tavern in the common room of the Tiger's Head Inn. He was also famished. He wondered if he needed to bring food for Deylia since neither of them had eaten all day but decided the priests would probably take care of all that.

Gondrial entered the inn's common room, and immediately his eyes rested on the massive mural above the bar of a giant tiger head. He glanced around the room and found a cozy little table off to one side. He went to the table and plopped down. A pretty girl with thick curly reddish-blonde hair met him at the table.

"What can I get you?" She said.

"An ale and whatever food is freshest," Gondrial replied. He leaned forward, "And the time you get done here." He winked.

"One ale, one stew and I will be spending time with my betrothed, Dorenn when I am done here."

"Shame, a pretty young girl like you attached already."

"I can see by the points on your ears that you are probably much older than you appear, and you appear to be pretty old."

"Ouch, I'm only half elfish. I'm not as old as you might think."

"Oh, in that case, I will go and get my grandma; she has been lonely lately."

"Are all women in Brookhaven as sharp-tongued?"

"I don't know. I don't know all the women in Brookhaven. I'll be right back with your stew." She walked away.

Gondrial leaned back in his chair. "Stew, why is it always stew? Can't these inns grill a nice steak or something?" He said to himself. "A potato is easy to bake in those stone ovens; one would think a nice roast chicken could be on the menu occasionally."

"You said it, friend." A burly man nearby said.

"Did I say anything to you...friend?" Gondrial asked.

"Forgive me. I was just being friendly. Why do you have such a chip on your shoulder?"

"I found out recently that I don't like burly men sitting around in inns."

The burly man made a derisive noise and turned back to his meal.

Just breathe, Gondrial. You don't want to fight or get kicked out of another inn. He thought.

A few moments later the pretty maiden brought his ale and food to him. He noticed that her shift was hiked up over her backside. "Ah miss," He began, "Your dress is hiked up. Here let me help you. He reached for the young woman's backside, fully intending to help her innocently.

The cloth covered wagon Rodraq had borrowed in Soldier's Bluff slowed and then jolted to a halt. Shey was perplexed. She leaned out the front opening and inquired, "Why did we stop?"

"My lady, there are highwaymen up ahead," Shey heard him say.

"Well, have they spotted us?" Shey asked.

"We're a bit difficult to miss, my lady." He said.

"Right," Shey said feeling a bit foolish. She looked at Sylvalora who was staring at her with a blank expression, "What?" Shey asked. The elvish woman said nothing so Shey continued, "We can't outrun them. I have to get them off our trail, and it's the only way."

"I was afraid of that," Sylvalora said. "You plan to use your essence magic. Essence cannot solve everything, dear, sometimes it just makes things worse."

Shey was blunt, "I suppose you have a better idea, then?"

"No, but I can't say I approve. What would you do if you had no magic to use? Shey said nothing. "You might use your head and live more by your wits. I have had magic in my soul for hundreds of years and how many times have you seen me rely on it when things got tricky?"

"Actually, a lot!"

"Really!" Sylvalora huffed.

"At least more than you believe you have." Shey reached for the clean linen wrap and opened the folds of fabric to view the sword. "We can't risk this being stolen."

"We aren't even sure it's Malinfel, Shey. I don't know why you insisted on removing it from the mantle after you saw the entire blade. That thing is beat up."

"It was attached to the mantle with a pretty powerful magic enchantment. Why would someone go to that much trouble if it wasn't significant? Besides, wasn't it you who insisted the sword was Malinfel in the first place?"

"I don't recall."

"Of course not, that's because it *was* your idea!" She re-wrapped the sword. It might not be Malinfel, or it might be, but I know it's significant either way. Once we get to Brookhaven, I will show it to Sanmir. He will know which sword it is, or if it's significant."

"My lady, the highwaymen are leaving."

"What?" Shey replied. "They are?"

"Aye, they are giving us a wide berth."

"Is this your doing?" Shey looked at Sylvalora.

Sylvalora shook her head, "I have done nothing."

Shey put the sword away and stepped to the driver's end of the wagon. Rodraq snapped the reins, and the wagon jolted forward once more. Shey stuck her head out the front flap again. The highwaymen were leaving the road and disappearing into the brush. "What the...I have never seen such a thing. One would think this wagon would be a prime target. It looks like a family traveling with all their belongings. One would think there might be something of value inside."

"Reputation," Sylvalora said. "This wagon must have already gained a reputation."

"I'm not sure there's been time for that. How would anyone know this was my wagon?" Shey asked.

The wagon rattled to a halt again. "Now what is it?" Shey said.

"My Lady, you might want to come out. I will put the steps down for you."

Shey looked at Sylvalora inquisitively and then stepped to the rear of the wagon where Rodraq was busy placing the steps for her. She stepped down on the wooden blocks and calmly crossed Rodraq and moved to the front of the wagon to get a better look. Rodraq waited with hand on sword. She noticed he had stopped and was staring at something directly ahead. When she moved to look at what held Rodraq's attention, she felt a lump form in her throat, something she was not accustomed of her throat doing. Partially camouflaged by its black and green scales and lying like a great cat across the whole of the road was a good-sized dragon. She had her head resting on her front claws, and she was staring intently at Shey.

"Rodraq, stay with the coach," Shey said. He tried to protest, but she waved him off. She approached the Dragon cautiously. It was obvious the dragon wished to speak with her, or she would not be laid out across the road blocking her path. "Hello?" Shey said sheepishly. Most of the dragons Shey had met were friendly to her due to her dragon affinity.

The dragon raised her massive head and let her tongue flicker out her mouth like a great reddish-brown ribbon, "Greetings Lady Shey of Symboria."

The two stared at each other awkwardly for a long moment before Shey spoke once again, breaking the silence, "Well, did you need to speak with me?"

"Such impetuousness why must you humans forever be in such a hurry?" She narrowed her eyes, "Forgive me, you are not quite human, are you?"

Shey chuckled, "So much for your perceptions. I am the very picture of humanity."

"Yes, well, if you insist dear. Who am I to judge?"

"Indeed." Shey couldn't help herself.

"I did want to speak with you, Shey of Symboria."

"Lady Shey" Shey corrected.

The dragon looked on with an amused expression but did not correct herself. "As I was saying, I do wish to speak with you." The scales around her mouth softened as she spoke and shimmered in the light changing from black to green and back again, "Why must our meeting be cold, distant, and hostile?"

"Changing the subject, are we?" Shey reacted.

"No, merely trying to lighten the mood. What I have to say is dark enough without all of the posturings."

Shey considered the dragon's words for a moment, "If you are looking for an amiable conversation that might be a bit difficult given that you may crush me or kill my friends with your size alone."

"Ahh, I see," said the dragon, "you speak to me so in order to prove your bravery in the face of overwhelming odds as a child may stand in defiance of his mother."

"More like a mouse might stand in defiance of a cat," Shey said just above a whisper.

"Very well. I am one of the Duil brood. I will even the odds for you."

"A shape changer?"

The Dragon shimmered and contorted until she was roughly the same size as Shey. She was human in appearance clothed in a dark green robe with golden accents. Her reddish-brown hair fell about her shoulders and complimented her sumptuous brown eyes. "Is this less threatening to you?"

"Amazing!" Shey said. "I never get used to seeing dragon shift no matter how many times I see it happen."

"You have seen it before?"

"Oh, yes, many times. It's impressive every time."

The dragon nodded, "I have come to you because you are one who can facilitate change. There is an abomination happening to my kith and kin that has not happened for some time. Some of my dragonkin have had their precious eggs stolen. You remember what happened some years ago?"

Shey hung her head low, "Aye, I remember. Toborne and Morgoran experimented with them, creating both Dramyd and Drasmyd Duil. I must confess, we have been made aware of possible Drasmyd Duil in the area, but I have heard nothing of Dramyds."

"Make no mistake; they are flying the skies once again. As you travel to Brookhaven, you will come across them at some point on the Southern Road. They were last seen just this side of Cedar Falls. They attacked someone."

"That's dire news. I'm sorry...I didn't catch your name?"

"My name is Chloranthe."

"Green Flower. Nice name."

"You know Dragon speech?"

"A small amount. I am sorry Chloranthe, but Toborne was destroyed by the Silver Drake, and Morgoran was cursed by her to see only possible futures forever. Neither could be manipulating dragon eggs anymore. I don't know who else would have the knowledge to create them."

"I am aware of both Morgoran and Toborne's fates. Morgoran's punishment is of particular interest since the curse is to force him to look at the possible consequences of his actions. However, there are followers of those two who could have resurrected the old ways."

"You know I'm an apprentice of Morgoran, and I assure you none of us followers are doing anything with dragon eggs. We find the secret experiments of our master just as barbaric as you. I'll say it again; I don't know of anyone who would venture back into those old experiments."

"What about Toborne's followers?"

"I can't speak for them or confirm if they even exist."

"They do, I'm afraid. It is good for me to hear how you feel. It leads me to believe I have come to the right person. I am asking you to find out who is creating the Dramyds and Drasmyd Duil and stop them once and for all. I want you to destroy any notes or remnants of the old ways and anything else that can be used to create the abominations."

"I would like to oblige you, but I am in the middle of another quest."

"I am aware of that quest as well. I believe my request and your quest will go hand in hand."

"Are you certain I am the right one to do this for you?"

"Aye, I am. You and yours can do this. There might be others as well, but I will leave that up to you to decide."

"Others?"

"As I said, your current quest and the one I give you go hand in hand."

Shey thought about what the dragon said, and she must have mistaken her pause for hesitation.

"If you do not wish to stop the abominations from being made in this world, we dragons will be forced to step in, and we will bring a war never before seen by human, elf, or dwarf kind before."

"Oh, no need for that. I will do as you ask. I will find out who is creating Drasmyd Duil and Dramyds. It isn't as if they are difficult to detect. The smell alone will alert me. You know, follow my nose to the culprits."

The dragon changed back into her dragon form, "Don't be so sure, lady of the Vale." She bellowed, "There have been changes." The dragon moved her massive wings, and the resulting wind shift nearly put Shey on her backside. The dragon lifted off and flew away toward the mountains.

"Changes? What changes?" Shey said to herself.

CHAPTER 16

ENCOUNTER AT BROOKHAVEN

Gondrial picked himself up off the street in front of the Tiger's Head Inn and dusted off the front of his tunic and pants. He was really beginning to loathe burly men in inns! He wasn't grabbing the girl's backside as everyone had misinterpreted. After a few moments contemplating whether or not to go back in and talk to the owners, he decided instead to go to the Grinning Goose Inn. It wasn't as nice as the Tiger's Head, but it was still a clean place to get a good meal and a soft bed. Besides, he would pass the Temple of Loracia on the way, and he could stop in and check in on Deylia.

Tarle was just coming out of the healing room when Gondrial entered the temple. "How is she?" Gondrial asked.

"We just got finished with our regimen. She reacted to it very well. We are hopeful for a full recovery. Although, you might have taken her to the Vale of Morgoran instead. She said you came from Cedar Falls."

"Brookhaven wasn't that far out of the way, and I have important business here."

"Business worth a girl's life?"

"Of course not. I have a few tricks up my sleeve. I wouldn't have let her get that far gone."

"I should hope not."

"Could I see her?"

"I don't see why not," Tarle said. "For a few moments only. Her body will need rest to heal properly."

Gondrial nodded and went to the healing room. When he entered, Deylia beamed. "Well, that's what I like to see. A big smile!"

"Thank you for getting me here, Gondrial."

"It was my pleasure. I'm just glad you are going to be okay."

Deylia looked at one of the women priests and then back at Gondrial, "I don't suppose you are free for the next few weeks after I am fully healed."

"I have business here, but it should conclude rather quickly. What did you have in mind?"

"Oh, what business? Nothing too pressing I hope."

"I'm meeting a friend who should be here at any time now. What did you need?"

"I need to get back to Trigothia. Since my father didn't make it and I am alone, I wondered if you might escort me home? I know it's asking a lot, but I don't think I could get back on my own."

Gondrial rubbed his chin. "You know, I get the feeling I will be heading back that way after I talk to my friend. I suppose I could get you at least as far as Seabrey where you could take the ferryboat across to Trigothia. That is, as long as you don't mind making a few stops along the way. I am kind of on a quest for my friend."

Deylia's face lit up. "I don't mind!"

"Good, I will see my friend, and you will heal up, and we will see where everything takes us from there." He glanced around, "I am starving. Are they feeding you here?"

"We will bring her food and drink." The priest nearby assured him.

"Good, I will be staying at the Grinning Goose if you need me."

"Oh, the Tiger's Head is nicer." The priest told him.

"So, I hear," Gondrial said with a smile. He put a comforting hand on Deylia's leg, "You hang in there. I will visit you again tomorrow."

Deylia nodded.

Gondrial left the room to see Tarle at the altar. He reached into his purse and removed two gold pieces. He placed them in the donation tin. "Take good care of her."

"Very generous of you. We will look after her with the utmost care. Of course, there is no need to donate. We will take care of her regardless."

"I know, but I don't expect you to burden yourself when I can pay."

Tarle nodded. "Perhaps I was too harsh – "

"Let me stop you right there. You were fine. I needed to hear what you had to say. I will be taking the girl home to Trigothia when she is healed. It is the least I can do for putting her in danger."

"Very decent of you."

Gondrial nodded. A few moments later he was rushing toward the Grinning Goose to get rid of his growling stomach.

Disguised as common travelers, Shey and Geron rode down from Watch Hill to the outskirts of the mountain village of Brookhaven. The midday sun was hot on their backs, but the crisp mountain air still kept them cool enough.

"Remember, Geron, while we are here you are pretending to be called Alwin, and I am your mother, Minda."

"I will remember."

"I mean it. Don't forget to call me Mother or Minda."

"I won't forget."

"That's a good boy. We don't want to draw too much attention to ourselves."

Sylvalora rode up behind them. "Don't forget me."

"Sylvalora will be called Aurelie," Shey told Geron.

"What of the wizard?" Geron asked.

Shey looked behind her as if she would see him riding up from behind. "He said he had an errand to run in Soldier's Bluff and he would be riding in behind us. I am not sure anyone knows him here in Brookhaven. As far I know, he will still be called Lyrrath."

At the gate, they were stopped by Thaq, the guard. Shey convinced him they were just weary travelers looking for a place to stay, and the guard let them pass.

Able to travel the streets of Brookhaven unmolested, Lady Shey rode directly for the apothecary shop to see Sanmir. She was hoping he could report on Marella's descendants.

When she arrived at the door, after tying up the horse and letting Geron down, she was met briefly by a boy with long brown hair and fierce, serious eyes. He took one look at Geron, blinked, and recoiled from him. Lady Shey was surprised to hear a horrified gasp from him.

"Excuse me, lad, is there something the matter?"

The boy regained his composure and stood up straight. "No, ma'am. I thought I saw something . . . I am not myself." He opened the door to the apothecary shop. "Are you going into the shop?"

"Aye, thank you." She took Geron's hand and walked through the door as the young man held it for her. He gave Geron considerable room to enter.

"Rennon, I thought you were in the storeroom. I have been calling for you. I need you to bring me some of the salve we made this morning," the man behind the counter instructed.

"How much?"

"About half a dram should do."

Lady Shey took the sword, still wrapped in cloth, to the counter and stood in line behind a plainly dressed woman with brown hair tied up in a bun. She eyed Sanmir cautiously to see if he would recognize her. He caught her gaze and gave her a friendly smile as she imagined he would like any other new customer. Sanmir's appearance didn't bother the inhabitants of Brookhaven. His dark skin, dark features, and slightly pointed ears pegged him as a sand elf from the kingdom of Darovan. Folks saw him as an exotic wiseman and trusted his legendary apothecary skills implicitly. His people were known for their potent cures and wonderous potions.

The boy Rennon returned with a dram vial and handed it to him. He looked at Geron with consternation. "I need the other preparation you make for me, sir, and I need it promptly, if you don't mind, sir."

Sanmir looked at him. "All right, where's the fire? I made some for you this morning. It's over there on the shelf." He said. The boy bolted to the shelf, took a small silver tin, and just promptly disappeared into the back storeroom.

As soon as the woman paid for her salve and left, Sanmir addressed Lady Shey. "Now that we are alone, what am I to call you this visit, my lady?"

"You do recognize me?" She was surprised.

"Maybe not at first. You fooled me for a moment or so."

"I am going by the name Minda, and this is my son, Alwin."

"Oh?" Sanmir was alarmed.

"He isn't really my son, Sanmir."

Sanmir was even more confused. "Why would you be traveling with a young boy? Is he part of..." he leaned forward, "our quest?"

"Not precisely, no, he is a young seer we . . ." Rennon entered the room again.

"Rennon, why don't you take the rest of the day off. I can handle the last two hours before we close. Go find Dorenn or Vesperin and enjoy yourself."

Rennon took another look at Geron, but this time he didn't seem as rattled by him. "Thank you, sir." He left the shop.

"Go on with what you were saying, my lady," Sanmir said.

"Geron, why don't you explore the shop for a moment but don't wander off."

"I'm Alwin."

"Aye, you're a clever boy." She rubbed his head and sent him off." When he wandered away, Shey addressed Sanmir again, "He's a seer that I have not seen do much seeing!"

"Oh, I see." Sanmir chuckled.

"I wasn't trying to be amusing."

"Never the less." He smiled.

Shey pursed her lips in disparagement, "I will speak of this young boy later. What do you have to report?"

Sylvalora entered the shop, and Sanmir bowed slightly to her.

"Don't bother bowing. Today, I am a simple peasant woman named Aurelie."

"Of course you are," Sanmir said.

"Come on now, Ger . . . er . . . Alwin, let's go get settled at the inn and let Mother and the apothecary talk." Sylvalora said. Geron followed Sylvalora out of the shop. Sylvalora whispered to Shey as she opened the door. "Meet us there when you are done." She walked out the door, letting it slowly come to a close behind her.

"A young seer boy?"

Lady Shey sighed. "We hadn't intended for him to travel with us this long. It just happened. He has a way of making you feel like he should come along."

"Ah, I understand. Well, you asked me for a report."

"Aye, go on."

"The boy Rennon you just met."

"Aye, what of him?"

"I think he is developing the wild magic. That tin he took brews a tea I made for him to suppress the ability. He isn't in danger of being detected by Enforcers yet. I will keep an eye on him and make sure he keeps from getting noticed."

"They sure do take outlawing magic seriously here in Symboria, don't they? Do the Enforcers come through here often?"

"Often enough, but I will keep him safe. The other boy, the descendant of Marella, his name is Dorenn, and he seems ordinary enough. If he can be taught to draw essence, it might be a tough task to get him started down that path. They are taught to fear and hate wielding here. In fact, parents use it to frighten the children. They tell them that if the children wander off, the wielders will get them and cast evil spells on them, keeping them from their parents forever."

"Oh, that's lovely."

"I said it might be difficult, but not impossible. I have overheard Dorenn talking to his friend Vesperin about it. It seems he has a fascination with wielders. It's a rebellious attitude some of the youth here have."

"They spoke of this out in the open?" Shey was shocked.

"Oh no. I was hidden when I overheard. The boys had no idea I was there. They thought they were in a secluded and secure place. When they sneak off on their own, that's when I find out the best information."

"I see. Is there anything else?"

"Not much of any importance, at least not yet. There is a half-elven lad called Trendan. He has lived in Brookhaven most of his life. By elvish standards, he's young. He has been acting like a big brother to Dorenn and his friends. Vesperin is a cleric of Loracia, and he keeps the others grounded and out of trouble most of the time. Oh, Gondrial is here. He ran into some trouble at the Tiger's Head Inn the other night and got himself thrown out. He is staying at the Grinning Goose now."

"Thank you, Sanmir. You have done a fine job keeping an eye on things here."

"My pleasure." He bowed.

"Try not to bow, dear. Remember, I'm merely a peasant."

"Hard habit to break, my lady."

"I understand. Here, what do you make of this?" She laid the sword onto the counter and unwrapped the cloth. She couldn't help but gasp when it was revealed. The sword had a faint orange glow it did not have before. "It's glowing?"

"Malinfel!" Sanmir said. "Where did you get this?"

"You won't believe it. We weren't sure it was Malinfel until this very moment."

"Well, it is, and something has triggered it." He bent down and whispered a few magic words and the sword sang out. He quickly recanted. "It does make a magic racket. It will have the Enforcers upon us if we aren't careful."

"What has triggered it? It was just an old, rusty arming sword until now."

"It's a mindwielder sword. Rennon has most likely triggered it with his wild magic. What are you even carrying it around for?"

"Morgoran told me to get it. He said it would aid us on our quest."

"Morgoran! You know better than that. He is cursed. You can't trust anything he says."

"I had a Lora Orbius. He was clear-headed."

"So what?" He has been cursed far too long to know what clear-headed is."

"Sanmir, I was there. He was fine for a time."

"I say get that sword out of Brookhaven and find a good hiding place. You shouldn't have it here of all places!"

Shey wrapped it back up in the cloth. "Do you have a place for it?"

"No, take it someplace and throw it down a deep hole. Somewhere you can get to it, but somewhere it can't cause you ill."

She gathered herself up. "Maybe you're right. I will find a good place for it."

"Good!"

"I best be off to find that fool Gondrial. I'm sure he has a few things to tell me." She grinned at Sanmir. "Or explain is probably more the case."

"Aye, if I think of anything else, I will let you know. I would say get that sword out of Brookhaven as soon as you are able."

"Very well. I will check in with you before I leave the village if I don't see you before then."

"Aye, and might I make one more suggestion." Sanmir held up his index finger.

"What is it?" she asked.

"You speak entirely too well for a peasant. You're not fooling anyone. Might I suggest you vary your speech a bit."

"You know, you're right. It's been so long since I had to use a disguise, I seem to have forgotten how. Thank you, old friend."

"Take care. I will be here if you need me."

Lady Shey acknowledged Sanmir, and a moment later, she was out the door.

"Now," she muttered to herself, "it's time for Gondrial to meet the business end of my boot! Then, I'll have him carry this sword off. He likes playing cat and mouse with Enforcers."

CHAPTER 17

WHISPERS OF THE WICKED

L ady Shey decided to check on Sylvalora and Geron before she
went traipsing over to the Grinning Goose after Gondrial. She
wanted to make sure her bags got to her room, and she thought she
might grab a bite to eat. She had a feeling she was going to need all of
her strength to deal with Gondrial.

At the door to the Tiger's Head Inn, Lady Shey noticed Lyrrath
slowly riding up to the inn's stables. Instead of going into the inn, she
decided to check on him. He had just handed over the reins of his horse
to the stable hand and removed his riding pack when she walked up to
him.

He turned into her as he left his horse. "Oh, I didn't recognize you."

"Shh!" She put her index finger to her lips. "Call me Minda. I am
just a regular peasant here." She spoke in a hushed tone.

Lyrrath leaned in. "Why the disguise?"

"The short version is I have interests in this village. The townsfolk aren't used to seeing lords and ladies here. I would draw too much attention to observe what I need to observe. I wanted to intercept you here before you saw me inside unaware."

"I see. You didn't want me calling out your true name in public."

She put the tip of her finger on the tip of her nose and winked.

"Fear not, I will keep to the secret."

"I apologize for not letting you know sooner, but you seemed preoccupied before we left Soldier's Bluff. Did you get your business concluded successfully?"

"I was, and aye, I did. I am not sure what came over me. I was so tired and fearful of every shadow. I went to a friend's house in Cedar Falls. She is a cleric of Loracia."

"And she channeled some healing for you?"

"Aye, and I feel much better now. No more fatigue."

"Good. Let's not linger here too long," she said. "I need to stow this package, and then I was about to get something to eat at the inn. Why don't you get checked in, and I will find Sylvalora and Geron. I am certain you must be hungry from the road."

"I am. What's the package?"

"Nothing special," she decided to downplay the sword's significance for Lyrrath's own good. "Just an old sword I need to get to Gondrial."

They entered the common room of the inn together. Lady Shey was immediately awestruck by the intricate mural of a giant tiger's head painted on the wall. She had seen it before, but it always impressed her each time she laid eyes upon it. Other than the mural, the common room looked about like any other she had seen, tables and chairs arranged in rows over a hardwood floor and a wood-trimmed bar along the back of the room for the maidens waiting on tables. A portion of the back bar doubled as a receiving desk for patrons in need of lodging.

Lyrrath went to the back desk to get a room, and Shey looked for a place to sit. As she searched around the room, she was surprised to spot Sylvalora and Geron. She waited for Lyrrath to return, and then she suggested they join the other two.

Just moments after they were seated and their orders for food were taken, Gondrial strolled in and directly located their table. Lady Shey could tell that at first Gondrial didn't recognize her. He had only seen Sylvalora. It wasn't until he sat down and introduced himself to Shey that recognition finally dawned on him.

"I am called Minda," Lady Shey said before he could get her name out. "Pleased to meet you."

"Charmed," Gondrial said, kissing her hand.

Shey leaned in and whispered to him. "I thought you got kicked out of here?"

"Kicked out, aye, but not banned. I was asked to leave actually. I am free to dine here," he whispered back.

"You know Lyrrath, do you not?" Sylvalora asked Gondrial.

"We have met." He extended his hand. "How are you, Lyrrath?"

"I'm well."

Sylvalora then indicated Geron. "This is Alwin, Minda's son."

Gondrial extended his hand to the boy, and they shook hands. Gondrial's expression soured. He yanked back his hand as if it was just in a fire. "I don't know where you all found this boy, but the kid's evil." He put his hand on the hilt of his sword.

"What are you doing?" Lady Shey whispered so loud she could have just said it in a normal tone.

"Look at him! That's not a boy; it's some kind of . . . of freak! He's one of *them*!"

"Gondrial!" Sylvalora said.

Lady Shey moved to Geron's defense as Gondrial stood to unsheathe his sword. For a moment, Geron seemed to flicker between a hideous black creature and the boy she knew. She shrieked, taken aback. The boy jolted up from his seat and hissed at Gondrial. In a flash, he weaved through the common room tables and was out the front door. Lyrrath was the first to chase after him.

Lady Shey grabbed ahold of Gondrial's arm. "How did you know?"

"A friend I met along the way cast some kind of spell on me. Apparently, it's still with me. Also, I imagine his illusion is weakening. How long has he been with you? Drasmyd Duil can only keep up an illusion for so long before they have to remake it."

"How can he be a Drasmyd Duil? There was no horrid stench or any of the other signs," Shey asked horrified.

"I don't know. I am about to find out. Lyrrath will catch him."

Shey had the sword leaning against her leg. "Here before you go. Take this sword."

"Why?"

"She put her mouth close to his ear, "It's Malinfel. Sanmir says to take it somewhere and hide it."

"Hmm," said as he took the sword grinning from ear to ear. "I have never had a mag- "

"Shh, not another word."

He glanced around the room just noticing it had gone silent. The handful of patrons were all aghast at what had just happened. One woman suddenly fainted and fell from her chair. "You had better take care of these people," Gondrial whispered to her. He took the sword and left the common room. Lady Shey and Sylvalora stood to get the attention of the startled patrons.

Geron ran behind the inn and headed for the cover of a few trees with dense bushes scattered around the thick trunks. He went ahead and let the illusion of the boy shift to his true form. He smacked his maw; it was good not to have to twist it into the flattened human form. His black scales glistened in the sunlight, so he used his ability to blend into the color of the bushes. He cursed himself for not renewing his changed form sooner. The one called Gondrial had only seen him because of carelessness; otherwise, the illusion was flawless, and he would never have been detected. He had come so far with the illusion.

He watched the inn intently from his position in the bushes. It appeared that only the one called Lyrrath pursued him. That would be a mistake. He conjured up bile from his stomach and held it in his mouth until Lyrrath was close enough, and then he leaped from the bushes and spat the acidic bile into Lyrrath's eyes and face. The man started to scream, but it quickly died off into a sickening gurgle as the man's face melted in the intense acid. Geron used his claws to stab the man in the chest repeatedly until he had soundly defeated him. He dragged the dead Lyrrath into the bushes. He used more of the black bile and kept coughing it up until he could cover the entire body with it. He watched with satisfaction as the body dissolved into the ground.

The Drasmyd Duil glanced up to see that Gondrial had exited the inn and was now searching nearby. He concentrated on his memory of Lyrrath and touched a fragment of bone that was still dissolving. The creature's face and body twisted and contorted into the perfect form of the dead man. He spit once more on the corpse to dissolve the rest of the clothing and stood up.

"Hey, over here. I caught up with it." His voice mimicked Lyrrath's exactly.

Gondrial hurried to him.

"There." He pointed to the putrid body dissolving into the ground. "I cast essence on him and stopped him, but when I caught up to him, he started doing that."

Gondrial went down to one knee. "I have never seen anything like this before. It seems he killed himself off. This is new. If he is a Drasmyd Duil, he is not one I have ever encountered before." He touched the tip of his finger to the ground, and it sizzled. He reached in his pocket and found a handkerchief. He concentrated on the fabric, and it glowed briefly with power. He used it to scoop up some of the liquid, dirt and all.

"What are you going to do with that?" Lyrrath asked.

"Take it to Sanmir. The Darovan elves have encountered a few creatures foreign to us here. He may have some idea of what it is we're dealing with." He took the sample and started walking toward the inn.

Shey and Sylvalora met him before he got too far.

"The patrons have no idea anything unusual happened," Shey told him. "It was horrible. We had that thing with us since Valwall and had no idea!"

Gondrial put his arm around Shey and handed the handkerchief to Sylvalora. "Here, take this to Sanmir if you don't mind. It's what remains of the creature. It apparently dissolved itself when Lyrrath caught up to it. It must be a new tactic."

Sylvalora carefully accepted the handkerchief.

Gondrial kept his arm around Shey's shoulder. "Come on; we will go to Sanmir's shop too."

Shey nodded.

"I am going to the inn to wash off. I think I got some of that . . . whatever it was on me. I will meet you at Sanmir's shop," Lyrrath said.

"All right, Lyrrath," Gondrial said as the three of them headed toward Sanmir's shop.

Lyrrath knew he had to complete his mission now, this moment, in case he was caught again. What if Sanmir knew how to detect him? He hurried to the inn and went inside. He made his way back to the bar at the back of the room and waited until he heard the name he was after. The big, balding man in the white apron behind the counter finally called it out. The boy named Dorenn appeared. The bald man sent him to the storeroom for a keg of ale. Lyrrath waited for his moment and then followed the boy. When he deemed it appropriate, he took the stone he had retrieved in the dungeons beneath the White Tower from his pocket and cast it at the boy, striking him in the back. A purplish flame covered Dorenn, and he fell to the floor. Lyrrath slinked away but not before he watched Dorenn get back up and go back to the common room. The boy was unaware. Lyrrath smiled.

That should suppress his ability to draw essence, he thought, *and if he does draw it in, he will have a sickness he will not soon recover from or forget!* Lyrrath walked through the common room. From what was left of Lyrrath's memories extracted from the dead man's essence, the creature thought of how Dorenn might behave if he did get essence sickness. *A bit whiny and even a bit annoying, perhaps?* The creature who was Lyrrath laughed to himself as he left the inn to join the others at Sanmir's shop.

CHAPTER 18

NO REST FOR THE DEAD

When they entered his shop, Lady Shey and Gondrial found Sanmir examining the contents of the handkerchief Sylvalora had given him. He was so intent that he didn't even look up when the small bell above his door jingled the arrival of potential customers. After a few moments, he retrieved an eyeglass and fastened it over his right eye.

He held the fabric and its contents up close to his eyeglass. "I will need to examine it in more detail and perform some experiments, but I believe it's a potent acid of some kind. I have some counter agents and salves that can negate it."

"There is no need for that. This was the boy who was traveling with us. Apparently, he was a shapeshifter, a form of Drasmyd Duil, perhaps. Have you seen anything like this before?" Sylvalora asked.

"Well . . . in Darovan, there is a species of flying Dramyd that spits acid similar to this, some kind of a cross between a drake and a desert lizard called a Firomanx. However, my people have supposedly killed off the brood."

"That doesn't mean the line could not have been reintroduced. There is evidence that Toborne and Naneden have continued the experiments of Kambor," Gondrial said.

Sanmir took off his eyeglass. "Kambor, the Oracle? He has been dead since the war."

Lady Shey sighed. "We have seen evidence he may just be dormant somewhere in The Sacred Land, possibly even revitalizing with The Sacred Land."

"I see. So that's why you came disguised for my report on the descendants of Ardenia. You have been reading the scattered, disjointed sketches of prophecy."

"Scattered and disjointed is correct. No one has ever taken the ramblings of Morgoran or the writings of the defeated Oracle seriously enough to research and record a true prophecy. Nevertheless, we are investigating all the possibilities."

"As you should be. What does Ianthill think?"

Gondrial chuckled. "We haven't gotten that far yet. I sure he still knows very little. I will send him a report as soon as I am able."

Sanmir put the handkerchief back down on the counter. "As far as I can tell, you brought this danger here with you. I have had no reports of Drasmyd Duil or Dramyds around Brookhaven. I shall double my efforts on watching Dorenn and his friends. It is possible this creature saw something or heard something. He might have made some kind of report before he died."

The bell above the door jingled, and Lyrrath walked in.

"Not likely," Sylvalora said. "He was in my sight the entire time."

Sanmir turned his attention to Lyrrath. "I understand you are the one who happened upon this creature. What happened?"

Lyrrath cleared his throat. "I chased the boy out behind the inn. I used essence and stopped him in his tracks near where he fell. When I caught up to him, he was spewing this substance from his mouth, and the rest of his body oozed it until he dissolved right before my eyes."

"You used magic here? A bold move considering the Enforcers are often seen around here," Sanmir said.

"I had to do something. I am not as young as I used to be. I couldn't let the boy get away."

Lady Shey was disgusted after hearing the details of the chase. "Enough. I don't want to discuss this anymore. I had grown fond of the boy, regardless, and I can't take hearing this again." She shoved off Gondrial, who was trying to offer comfort and headed for the door. "It's been a long day. I am going to find the inn mistress, get some overpriced elvish wine, and go to my room."

Sylvalora smoothed down her robes. "I think I will join her."

As soon as Sylvalora left the shop, Gondrial locked the door behind her and let the cloth shade fall with the word *closed* printed on the outside of it.

"Gondrial, it isn't—"

"You're closed!" He pulled a bottle of mountain-distilled whiskey out from under his leather vest.

"Aye, I believe I am. I will get the glasses. There is a table in the black room."

"Pull up a chair, if you can find one, Lyrrath. It's time to leave your worries at the door and float on the whiskey river." He watched Lyrrath retrieve a chair. "You seem different somehow."

Lyrrath froze for a moment and then pulled up the chair, "Oh, how so?"

"I think your ordeal might have put you in dire need of some liquid medication."

Lyrrath's face lit up, "Aye, I do believe so."

Gondrial poured the drink the glass Sanmir had brought to the table. The extra sword he had at his side burned enough so that Gondrial had to lean it against the leg of the table. He smiled at Lyrrath trying not to give away what he was seeing, the hideous face fluctuating before him as the spell Deylia had cast on him began to wear off.

After breakfast, Lady Shey decided it was time to leave before someone realized she no longer had a son. It was time to get back to Soldier's Bluff and Rodraq, who had taken the borrowed wagon back the night before. Gondrial had sent a nearly fully recovered Deylia along with him. Sanmir arranged for Shey and Sylvalora to each have a horse, which would be returned to Brookhaven by the stablemaster at Soldier's Bluff once they left in the coach. The only danger in Brookhaven was the danger she had brought with her. Ianthill was right; Sanmir was a fine choice for guardian, and the Darovan elf enjoyed being the village apothecary. At the stables, she watched Gondrial fumble with his bridle, obviously recuperating from last night's drink. It was probably a good thing to get him away from Brookhaven as well before he did more damage than good. Behind Gondrial, an unusually quiet Lyrrath prepared his horse.

"Are you ready to ride out, Minda?" Sylvalora asked.

"I'm ready, Aurelie."

Shey thought by having Sylvalora ride out of the village with her that anyone who remembered her riding with someone might forget it was originally a little boy. After they put some distance between them and Brookhaven, she relaxed. Gondrial and Lyrrath were to catch up with them after Watch Hill.

It was late afternoon, nearly evening when the four of them reached the sprawling town of Soldier's Bluff. They rode directly to the Sea and Ale Inn, where they found Rodraq having his supper in the common room after they had their horses stabled and their things taken up to their rooms. Shey and Sylvalora remained dressed in their plain clothing when they entered the common room. Almost immediately after supper, Lyrrath excused himself, so the remaining four went out into the private balcony to fill in Rodraq on the events of Brookhaven and discuss their next move.

Rodraq drew heavily on his pipe and let the white smoke drift from his lips. "When I noticed the boy didn't come in the common room with you, I thought maybe he had been held up stabling his horse or something, at first."

Gondrial must have seen the distress on Shey's face. "This has become a sore subject for Lady Shey, Rodraq. I think she would rather move away from it."

Shey nodded.

"Forgive me, my lady; I wasn't thinking," Rodraq said.

"How is the girl?" Sylvalora asked.

Gondrial took out his pipe and began to fill it. "I'm going to have to visit the tabac shop tomorrow. I'm nearly out."

"Gondrial, Sylvalora asked you a question," Shey said.

"Hmm? Oh, my apologies, the girl is still recovering. She is sleeping right now, and I expect her to stay in bed until we leave. Nasty stuff, Dramyd poison." He finished stuffing his pipe.

"Soldier's Bluff has some fine blends of tabac from the fields near here," Rodraq said.

"I have heard. I am looking forward to trying some." Gondrial answered.

"Go ahead, Gondrial. I know you want to. I don't mind this time," Shey said.

Gondrial was confused. "The shops are closed, and I still have some of my tabac from Symbor."

"No, not the tabac. I saw you eyeing the ale drafts on the way up. Why don't you and Rodraq go and get you a pint and bring it up here? In fact, I think Sylvalora and I would enjoy an elvish wine as well."

"I knew there had to be an ulterior motive," Gondrial said.

"Are you complaining?" Shey asked, sitting up slightly in her seat.

"Oh no, no, I'm not. Come on, Rodraq."

The warrior put his pipe down on the wooden arm of his chair. "You'll watch this for me?"

"Aye, we won't let it get away," Shey said.

"What did you want to say to me?" Sylvalora said as soon as Rodraq left.

"What?" Shey said absently.

"I thought you sent the boys away on purpose, to talk to me in private, perhaps."

"No, not this time. After the events in Brookhaven, I thought the last thing I needed to be was ridged and controlling. Let the men relax and have some fun for a little while."

"Sheyna Namear, you are not fooling me. You know something or feel something. Is it about the boy?"

"Maybe, I don't know. When Ianthill took over for Morgoran as my master, he tried to tell me a day would come when The Sacred Land would renew its power, and there would be a struggle to get at that power. I just didn't know I would be so vested in all of it. A guardian of the descendants of my best friend, a master wielder, now maybe a mentor to those descendants. Dark days are ahead, and I thought maybe Gondrial, Lyrrath, and Rodraq could use some slack before they become frontline soldiers."

Gondrial and Rodraq returned with two pints, a bottle of wine, and two wine glasses. To be polite, Gondrial opened and poured the wine before he took his seat and resumed preparing his smoking pipe. He turned his padded seat to face out over the balcony. He was about to light his pipe when he saw Lyrrath walk from the rear of the inn toward a heavily wooded area.

"Shey, is that Lyrrath?" He pointed to the man walking across the rear lawn of the inn.

"I do believe it is," Lady Shey agreed. "Shall I call to him?"

"No, let him go. I want to see where he ends up."

Rodraq squinted to see in the dark. "Did he go into the woods? I wish I had your elvish eyesight!"

Gondrial got up from his chair. "He is about to go into the woods, and he is stopping to look around. That's not the look of a man who is out for a night stroll; that's the look of a man who is checking to see if he is being followed."

Lady Shey gasped as Gondrial flipped over the balcony and carefully climbed down the rock-sided building to the ground. "Be careful, you fool," she said.

"I will be right back," he whispered up to her.

They all hurried to the edge of the balcony to watch Gondrial silently stalk across the lawn and enter into the woods at the precise spot Lyrrath entered.

Gondrial caught up to Lyrrath and followed him deeper into the woods. He remembered the overly cautious and paranoid Lyrrath and wondered why it was suddenly so easy to follow him. The Lyrrath he knew would have known he was on his heels. But this was not eh Lyrrath he knew. It was the Drasmyd Duil, and he was up to something. This was the moment Gondrial had been waiting for. He had to restrain himself from drawing, in essence, to cloak himself from the other man's perceptions. Since Lyrrath was also a wielder, he presumed, he might detect the flow of power around him this close. Being half-elven, Gondrial was pretty light on his feet, anyway, when he needed to be. He came within listening distance and promptly found a place to hide and listen. *Who is Lyrrath talking to anyway? Himself?*

"Why do you summon me here? It is dangerous. I was almost caught once already," Lyrrath said.

"The true master prepares in The Sacred Land. He sends me."

Gondrial could not see the other figure well, but judging by its guttural voice and thick speech, he knew what it was, another Dramyd Duil. Why was the fake Lyrrath meeting with such a creature? His first impulse was to confront them. He had replaced his usual sword with Malinfel, and the sword was heating up again. Gondrial pulled the blade an inch out of the scabbard. It was glowing a faint orange color.

"Tell the master I have completed my first mission," Lyrrath said.

"I will not be going back to the master. I have a mission of my own. I am only here to convey your next mission."

Abruptly, it dawned on Gondrial. The creatures were probably planning something terrible like trying to intercept Shey's coach. He was also sickened when the realization came to him that the thing did something back in Brookhaven and completed his mission.

"Our master has had another vision from his tomb. You are in a position to kill the one known as Lady Shey, but you are to leave the one called Sylvalora alive. I have business in Brookhaven. The master has confirmed the one called Dorenn will one day be able to control the vast power of The Sacred Land once it completes its renewal cycle. I will see him dead."

"I should go. The others will grow suspicious. But first, I must ask how you will gain access to the village? You do not have the visage of someone who can gain easy access to the boy as I do. I should go back to the village. I can easily make up a story to get away from the others."

"No, you are to kill the woman, and there is more to your mission. I have a way into the village. I will be ready to leave tomorrow. The master says after you kill the woman, you should travel to Symbor and meet Naneden. The grimoire with the traveling spells is located there. You will help him steal it from the king's palace." Two wings extended up in the air behind the creature. "I smell something. Someone is near." It flapped its wings and took off into the night sky. Lyrrath began to sniff the air. Gondrial backtracked a few steps and then decided it would be better to feign ignorance and confront the creature right then and there. He came stumbling up near where the two creatures were meeting. He began to unbutton his pants as if he was about to relieve himself. He appropriately jolted when he saw Lyrrath.

"Lyrrath," he slurred, "you frightened the fire out of me. What are you doing out here wandering the woods this time of night?"

"The same as you. I needed to take a break."

"Well, I can't go now. You scared it right back in. I better have some more ale." He turned back toward the inn. "You had better do your business and get out of these woods. Dangerous creatures prowl around out here." He began to stagger back the way he came.

He started singing a drinking song to hide his nerves. He heard the imposter walking behind him.

"If there are creatures out here, your singing will repel them!"

Gondrial smiled to himself. *That's something Lyrrath would have said. This new Drasmyd Duil is a clever deceiver.*

CHAPTER 19

BORN OF EVIL

G ondrial wondered if Lyrrath was going to try to carry out his mission immediately. He hoped he had time to warn Shey about the imposter first.

"Wait a moment, what am I thinking!"

"What was that?" Lyrrath asked.

Gondrial faced Lyrrath. "I don't have to warn Shey."

Lyrrath looked confused, and Gondrial was amused by it. Raising his hands to chest level, Gondrial began to draw in essence while a simultaneous bluish-purple ribbon of pure essence formed behind him, writhing back and forth and moving in circles like an ethereal snake. "I think this deception has gone far enough. Once I get rid of you, I will send Shey and Sylvalora back to Brookhaven to kill your friend."

"You talk too much, Gondrial. What are you doing? Essence will alert Enforcers. You forget where you are."

"Good, let them come. I need something to combat that acid of yours. Where do you squirt it out from?"

Lyrrath assumed an attack posture, his mouth expanding too far to be human. As Gondrial prepared the essence ribbon, the imposter spit out his acid bile. With a flick of the wrist, the ethereal ribbon of essence hovering above Gondrial intercepted the acid, eliminating it.

"Nice try, Drasmyd Duil. So, this is how you killed Lyrrath. You can drop the illusion."

The illusion of Lyrrath faded away, revealing the dark, leathery skin and scales of a Drasmyd Duil. It spoke in a deep, guttural voice.

"You had better pray to Fawlsbane Vex or Loracia that there are no Enforcers nearby. That ribbon of essence must scream of your presence."

"Yep, I'm certain. You just let me worry about the Enforcers, and you worry about me!" Gondrial reached out with lightning speed, his forefingers, and middle fingers at a point on each hand. The ribbon of essence followed his movements. Each time the tips of his fingers touched the torso of the Drasmyd Duil, the essence ribbon followed and struck at exactly each point where his fingers had just been. The Drasmyd Duil screamed as each essence strike became a piercing sword wound. It tried to spit, and Gondrial again blocked it with essence. The Drasmyd Duil lurched forward, and Gondrial pushed it back, the essence ribbon following through at each touch. Gondrial kicked out with his leg to unbalance the monster, and the Drasmyd Duil went down on one knee. He clasped the creature's head with both hands and released. The essence ribbon came in force from both sides and penetrated its head, snaking through and exiting the mouth. The creature collapsed to the ground, and Gondrial let the ribbon dissipate. He drew Malinfel and thrust the glowing orange blade into the creature's back. The orange of the blade slid off into the creature, and it writhed violently before becoming still with death. He wiped the blade clean with his handkerchief and sheathed Malinfel.

"Not such an improved version of Drasmyd Duil, after all," he said. "I had better get you a little farther into the woods. I don't have time to bury you, and I'd wager it won't take you long to start stinking. Thunder and rain! Who am I talking to? You're dead!" He kicked the creature in the side. "That's for making me talk to myself." He went to the head of the creature and started pulling it back into the woods by its leathery wings. "That kick was for Lyrrath too."

Once he hid the carcass sufficiently far enough into the woods, he rushed back to the inn. He hadn't taken five steps out of the woods before he saw two men in black cloaks searching near the edge of the woods directly south of him. He took off in the opposite direction, avoiding them. *There are Enforcers in the area!* He thought. *Just my luck. It's only a matter of time before they find the corpse.* He made his way back inside and up the stairs to Sylvalora and Shey, who were waiting anxiously for him.

"I felt essence," Lady Shey said. "What happened?"

"You weren't the only one. There are two Enforcers searching about."

"Where is Lyrrath?" Sylvalora asked.

"On the ground outside of the Tiger's Head Inn and in Sanmir's shop back in Brookhaven, I should think. Killed by that Drasmyd Duil. It's some kind of new version, better at disguise, no stench to give it away, and some deadly spit. It wasn't very good at fighting me off. I dispatched it."

"And you drew the attention of the Enforcers," Sylvalora said.

"Well, I had the feeling that a sword or a dagger probably wouldn't be able to repel deadly acid spit!"

"It's of no matter now. The deed is done," Shey said.

"There was a meeting in the woods with another Drasmyd Duil. The other one plans to go to Brookhaven. The one I killed was supposed to go to Symbor and help Naneden steal a tome from the king's library that contains travel spells right after it killed you first, Shey. The enemy also knows about the descendants of Ardenia."

"What did you do with the one you killed?" Sylvalora asked.

"I dragged it into the woods. It's a good bet; the Enforcers will find it very soon."

"They have ways of tracing essence use back to the user."

Gondrial nodded, "Aye, I realize that, Sylvalora. I have to leave now, tonight."

Lady Shey began to gather up her things. "We have to get back to Brookhaven."

Sylvalora agreed. "All right, here's what we are going to do. Gondrial, you will go to Symbor and find out what you can about Naneden and the travel tome there. If you find him and can stop him, do so. Shey and I will take care of the Drasmyd Duil in Brookhaven. Who will it be disguised as?"

"It didn't come up. The creature said it would find a way."

"Will the girl be all right to travel?" Shey asked.

"She should be. I told her there might be side trips on the way to Trigothia." Gondrial said.

"Shey, gather up your things. Rodraq, get the coach ready while we pack. We will drop all pretenses and take the coach to Brookhaven, which means you should travel as Lady Shey now. We actually want your reputation to precede us now. It might be useful." Sylvalora said.

Gondrial gave Shey a curt hug, and then he did the same with Sylvalora.

"Good luck, Gondrial. I will send word from Brookhaven, and we will meet you in Symbor," Shey said. As an afterthought, she added, "If you find yourself with free time, stay out of the taverns!"

"You know me. I'm all work." Gondrial's sly smile was not convincing.

Shey was clearly not amused. "It's no joke. You know what Naneden is capable of, and you will need to keep a good head on your shoulders if you have a run-in with him."

Footsteps, like heavy boots on bare wood, reverberated from the hallway. They stopped, and a knock came at the door.

"Who's there?" Sylvalora called out.

"Enforcers, ma'am. Please open the door."

Gondrial tiptoed toward the balcony. "That was fast! Open the door, and I will lead them off. Get to Brookhaven!"

"Wait, hide," Shey waited until Gondrial hid off the edge of the balcony, making sure the Enforcers couldn't see him before she opened the door. Shey embraced the first Enforcer before the door completely opened. "Thank Loracia you are here." She pointed to the balcony, "There he goes, the fiend! He jumped down just now. You must go after him."

"Who ma'am?"

"That horrible man who has been holding us hostage in our own room by force."

"You might be able to catch him if you hurry," Sylvalora added.

Both Enforcers ran back down the hall and to the stairs. Gondrial popped back up from the side of the balcony as soon as they were gone. "Good, a pair of bright ones. This should be fun!"

CHAPTER 20

DRASMYD DUIL

L ady Shey and Sylvalora met Rodraq in front of the inn. Lady Shey was worried when she didn't see the coach. Gondrial had already saddled the horses and slipped out of town with Deylia. He made sure to cast a few spells in order to get the Enforcers on his trail and to draw them away from the corpse in the woods. If they had found it, Enforcers would descend from all around, making it difficult for Shey and Sylvalora to travel to Brookhaven and take care of business. The last thing they needed was a collection of Enforcer checkpoints sprouting up and down the Southern Road.

"The stable hands are still hitching up the horses. They will pull the coach around when they are through," Rodraq said as if he read Shey's worried expression.

While they were waiting, Shey noticed the local peddler's wagon rumbling along on the cobblestone street. As it passed, she made eye contact with the peddler. He smiled and gave her a friendly salute by mimicking tipping a hat, even though he wore none, which was a common form of a wave in the kingdom of Symboria. Still, she got a chill that turned into an ill feeling.

Their coach pulled up, and Rodraq began to load Shey and Sylvalora's belongings. Shey could hear a squeaking sound, so she went to where Rodraq was finishing his task. She noticed one of the rear wheels had begun to creak and groan. She looked at Rodraq.

"Aye, I hear it too." He examined the rear spokes, tugging on them. One of the bottom spokes pulled apart, followed by another. "At least two spokes have been sawed in half." He went around the coach, testing each wheel. Spokes had been sawed in half on each of them. "All of the wheels on this coach are useless. Once the coach got up to speed, they would each give way." He lamented.

Lady Shey addressed the nearest stableman. "You there, who is the wheelwright?" He pointed to a man already examining the wooden wheels. Shey went to him. "How long would it take to repair?"

The man peered up at her. "With help, about a day, two by myself."

"That's outrageously long! I wouldn't think it would take more than a few hours."

"If you want it done right, my lady, where they won't come loose easily on the rough road, it takes time."

"What about new wheels? Do you have them in stock?"

"I believe so, but that would be much more expensive."

"But it would be faster, right? You could get a few men together to work on changing each wheel."

"I suppose I could. What's your hurry, my lady?"

"Do it. The cost is of no consequence, and you let me worry about the urgency of my departure." She stepped into the coach and returned with a bag of gold pieces. She handed them to the wheelwright. "This is more than enough. Get to work right away, please."

The wheelwright's eyes brightened. "I shall get these changed at once." He grabbed the reins of the lead horse and led it to his shop.

"What is it, Shey?" Sylvalora asked.

"That peddler. There was something wrong with him. It's just a feeling. I think he sawed our spokes so that he would have a head start."

Sylvalora lowered her voice. "You think he might have been hiding something? Do you think he was the other creature Gondrial saw?"

"I don't know. Gondrial never got a look or notion at who the other creature would be disguised as. I know at this point is we need to get to Brookhaven and assume the worst, that there is another shapeshifter as good as the one Gondrial killed in the woods with a head start."

"Aye, anyone could be a suspect."

"I agree, but still, I can't exactly just run up and jab a dagger into anyone I suspect. In the old days, other than the horrible smell they gave off, Drasmyd Duil could be detected by mindwielders. There are still a handful of them around."

"Mindwielders that know how to control their power are significantly rare, my dear. However, I do know of two, but they are both in hiding."

"There is another, and he is close by, but he is untrained and untested."

Sylvalora smoothed back her hair. "The boy Sanmir told you about with the wild magic. Do you believe he is a latent mindwielder?"

"Aye, I do."

"All right, but we will have to bring out his power slowly and carefully."

The coach almost felt like it was gliding on its new wheels. At the behest of Lady Shey, Rodraq had purchased two more horses for a total of four to help pull it, and he was running them moderately fast. Two soldiers from Lux Enor on white steeds showed up just before they departed for Brookhaven, looking for Lyrrath, who had failed to report his progress. Shey explained what had happened to him and recruited them to ride along and add to the mystique of a noblewoman wielder traveling through territory where magic was outlawed, but where no one, not even Enforcers, would try to detain her for it. The two men wanted to investigate the area of Lyrrath's disappearance in Brookhaven, anyway, so they readily agreed to escort her coach.

Maintaining a rapid pace, it still took them almost to Brookhaven to catch sight of the slower moving peddler's wagon ahead. The peddler must have seen them and picked up the pace a bit because once they had spotted him, the distance between them remained about constant.

Shey climbed up into the driver's seat with Rodraq to get a better view. They had begun to close the gap between them when Shey saw movement from the corner of her eye. Something dark was moving extremely fast through the trees to her right. She watched the woods and evergreen for a while, but the shadow was gone. She lowered herself back down into the coach.

"There is a shadow moving rapidly through the trees, matching our speed," she told Sylvalora.

"Then the peddler isn't the Drasmyd Duil."

"I don't know. That thing I saw could be something else. It doesn't have to be the creature Gondrial saw. The peddler could be harboring something in his wagon."

"My lady, we are catching up to the peddler. He appears to have stopped off to the side. Shall I pass him on the road or stop?" Rodraq called down.

Shey pulled the coach window down and leaned out slightly. She could see the wagon and two youths climbing onto it. "Someone is joining the peddler," she said to Sylvalora.

"My lady?" Rodraq called down to her.

"Pass them so I can see who has joined the peddler, and then stop," Shey instructed.

The peddler's wagon jolted and began to move, but Shey's carriage was moving faster, and Rodraq passed them. Shey and Sylvalora could now see the two young people riding on the wagon.

Sylvalora put her hand lightly over her mouth. "You have to go out there and stop him. I recognize the boy as Dorenn Adair. That peddler is trying to take them off to that creature."

"Are you sure? You don't believe he is a Drasmyd Duil?"

"No, I really don't. I think he is a pawn. Otherwise, he wouldn't have waited on us to catch up to him. He would have just killed Dorenn and flown away in triumph. I think this is a simple coincidence. I think the peddler was supposed to get into the village and bring him out."

"I see. I will be right back," Shey said.

Rodraq lowered the steps, opened the coach door, and extended his hand to help Lady Shey out of the coach.

The End of book 1: *Shadows of Yesterday*

Book 1: *The Harrowing Path* begins the Story of Dorenn Adair.

Afterword

This is a second edition of the prequel story. I wanted to bring this story up to date so it fits better with the second editions of the rest of the series. If you have bought this book with the temporary cover of the girl with the sword, congrats! Hold on to it because it will be a collector's edition. I plan to change the cover to match the rest of the series in the near future. If you have the book with the new cover, don't worry, it's the same book. I hope you enjoy the series!

ALSO BY CLEAVE BOURBON

Tournament of Mages Series:

Red Mage: Ascending Book 1

Blue Mage: Equinox Book 2

Black Mage: Cursed Book 3

Green Mage: Metamorphosis Book 4

Grey Mage: Protector Book 5

White Mage: Rhapsody Book 6

Enter the Arena Book 7

Prequel The Seventh God

Shadows of the First Trine Series:

Book 1 The Harrowing Path

Book 2 Serpent in the Mist

Book 3 Seer of Shadows

Book 4 Undead Inheritance

Book 5 Fury of the Lich

Prequel Shadows of Yesterday

War of the Oracle Series:

Dragon's Blood Book 1

The Cursed Phylactery Book 2

Wizards of War Book 3

Lurker in the Shadows Book 4

GLOSSARY

Adracoria - Southernmost Trigothian kingdom. Ruled by the Adrac
f   a   m   i   -
ly.

Aedreagnon – (a-dray-ag-non) One of the eight gods. First son of
Fawlsbane Vex and Loracia. He never did have the creative sense and
the drive of purpose like his younger siblings. Instead he was jealous of
their creative genius and often used their creations to make followers
of his own (Dramyds and Drasmyd Duil out of dragons, etc.) He
would also teach his disciples to do the same. His jealously tended to
make people misunderstand him and label him as evil.

Ageanna - One of the eight gods. Creator of drakes and dragonkind. Youngest female child of Fawlsbane Vex and Loracia. Fawlsbane loved her creation of dragons so much he made his own (golden
and silver dragons) and even created dragons to guard the realm of the
gods, Venifyre.

Amadace - Dragon in which Bren serves as First Knight.

Amalease Stone - Stone used to gain entry into the gates of Drae-godor. It is located on Mount Urieus.

Amar - Race of high men from Lux Amarou. First creation of Fawlsbane Vex.

Anisport - Largest port city of Denosia, across the Great Sea.

Arasyth/Sythia - Trigothian kingdom between Adracoria and Ardenia, host to the Great Sythian Forest. Ruled by the Arasyth family.

Ardenia - Northernmost Trigothian kingdom. Ruled by the Arden family.

Arillian Elves - High elves from the Isle of Arillia. They migrated to the Isle of Arillia at the end of the first age after their forests became grasslands and the area now known as Ishrak had become cursed. They are the fairest of elves and most elegant.

Are'dune - Race of men who can trace their origins to Lux Amarou and the Amar but are not considered truly high men.

Ascendic Root - A potent root made into a tea and drank. It relieves pain depending on the dose. Higher doses cause euphoria. Weak tea relieves the minor pain of headaches, etc., while strong tea relieves severe pain.

Asheth's Grimoire - An ancient tome containing spells of essence used to travel magically over distances. It is believed that Migarath used spells from the grimoire as a basis to build his famous Migarath Portals. (See Migarath Portals.)

Bannon, Ezra - A powerful mindwielder and ally to Toborne. Also the reeve of Briarwick, Adracoria.

Basillian - One of the great port cities in the kingdom of Symboria. Basillain is located in Northern Symboria, south of Seabrey. Due to disputes and treaties, Basillain is the port city in the north for trade with Adracoria. Seabrey is the northern port city for trade with both Ardenia and Sythia.

Bittering Tea - A strong brew made from the grinding of the bittering bean. It has a distinct aroma and is usually consumed in the morning as a stimulant.

Breannan - One of the eight gods. Oldest daughter of Fawlsbane Vex and Loracia, co-creator of the race of elves, lover of trees, nature and things that grow.

Bren - Dragon knight from Draegodor. First Knight of Amadace.

Brendlewyre - See Theosus Fiderea.

Broodlord - Common name given to a dragon knight with high ranking. (A brood is a family of something. A broodlord would be a high member of a family or lord of the brood.)

Brynna - An Arillian, elf maiden, healer. She is the eldest daughter of Erinthill, and Ianthill's niece. She resides on the Isle of Doom (Rugania).

By'temog - The largest city of Ishrak, it was once the kingdom's capital city. It fell into ruins after the curse of General Sythril. The general is currently trapped as a ghost there, lurking among the ruins.

Chamber of Ancients - An ancient room in the citadel of Rugania (the Isle of Doom) where youthful wielders take part in magical trials. It is also a place to cure essence sickness if necessary.

Darovan - Island continent southwest of the tip of Adracoria where some of the elves of old migrated. Home to the Siladil and Noradil elves.

Delanora/Delanorasylva - Dragon-speak name for Shadesilver.

Dellah – Former Inn mistress of the Tiger's Head Inn in Brookhaven, Symboria. Currently the queen of the Trigothian kingdom of Ardenia, Mother to Dorenn Adair.

Denosia - Mysterious kingdom on the continent across the Great Ocean.

Deylia - A young Trigothian woman who befriends Rennon in the capital of city of Trigoth.

Dorenn Adair - Innkeeper's son from the village of Brookhaven in Southeastern Symboria. Son of Lourn and Dellah Adair.

Draegodor (*Dray-go-door*) - The city of red. Home of the dragons not in exile, nestled deep in the Jagged Mountains.

Dragon Claw - Parrying sword (dagger) of a dragon knight. Not actually a dragon claw but made of metal.

Dragon Fang - Sword of a dragon knight. Not actually a dragon fang but made of metal.

Dragon Knight - Men, elves, dwarves, and Scarovs who have chosen, or have been chosen by the dragons, to serve as knight protectors of the dragon realm.

Drakkius - Symbolic leader of Abaddonia.

Dramyd (*Draw-mid*) - Winged creature created from drake eggs. Designed to kill, they do the bidding of Aedreagnon, Drasmyd Duil, Naneden, and Toborne.

Dranmalin/Draenmaulin - An ancient sword forged by dragons. Its name literally means dragon hammer in ancient dragon-speak. It magically binds to its owner. It is currently Dorenn Adair's sword after leaving Signal Hill.

Drasmyd Duil (*Draws-mid Do-ill*) - Shapeshifters. They are cunning and deadly. They usually lead packs of Dramyds. They are also known as Shadow Lurkers. They answer to Toborne.

Duil Clan - Clan of dragonkind Toborne used to create the Drasmyd Duil. Their specialty is shape-shifting into other beings.

Endil - (Foreshome) Home city of the wood elves (Sylvan, Eridil) located deep in the Great Sythian Forest.

Elanadil - Name of the magical sword of Ianthill. (It is a purely conjured sword.)

Elvander - Name of the magical sword of Seancey Namear.

Enowene (*IN-O-ween*) - Arillian elf and younger sister of Ianthill and Erinthill.

Eridil - Elven name for wood or Sylvan elves. They are the only race of elves that did not migrate; instead, they made their home in Endil (Foreshome), where they still remain. They are shorter than Arillian elves and have slightly darker skin, but are still considered fair and wise.

Erinthill - Arillian elf and fraternal twin sister of Ianthill, mother of Brynna.

Essence Sickness - An illness caused by the unskilled use of drawing essence for magical purposes. It usually occurs to first-time wielders who have yet to be trained. It does not occur, however, if the wielder discovers he can draw essence as a child (before puberty). The illness is characterized by wild mood swings, delusions of grandeur, and eventually insanity. If left untreated, the insanity will be followed by death. Wielders afflicted with essence sickness often speak uncharacteristically of themselves, and say things they would never say otherwise.

Fawlsbane Vex - God, co-creator of the world, and father of the gods. Husband of Loracia, Goddess of Life.

Ganas Nashe (*Gann-is Na-shae*) - Scout from Brookhaven for the king's army of Symboria. Finder of the Lost Army in Denosia.

General Rellagorn - Leader of the army of the North and West.

General Sythril - General of Sythia who fought in the Ishrakian war. He hired seers to curse the leader of Ishrak so he could win. When the seers cursed Ishrak, they warned him not to follow the beaten army, but he didn't listen. He pursued the opposing army back into Ishrak in order to defeat them unconditionally. Unfortunately, he led his army into a doomed land where he eventually became part of the curse he created.

Golvashala - A golden dragon also known as the Oracle. Golvashala means gold scales in dragon-speak. He is the cause of the War of the Oracle that created the Sacred Land. He is also called Kambor in common tongue.

Gondrial - First apprentice to Ianthill. A longtime friend of Lady Shey.

Hadder - An apothecary in Trigoth who brews potions that affect the mind.

Ianthill (*E-un-thill*) - Member of the holy trine (First Trine) representing elves Xeian, and Breannan. (Favors ruling with compassion, kindness, and a people's majority.)

Imprints/Imprinting - The act of putting matching images, etc., magically into skin. Some cultures do this to signify marriage in which the imprints serve where gold or other precious metals made into rings might serve in other cultures.

Ishrak - Northern kingdom bordering Symboria, the Jagged Mountains, and Ardenia. The kingdom was cursed and remains a forbidding, desolate land full of danger. Only small pockets of man, elf, and civilized folk live there.

Jac - Member of the lost army.

Jungle Elves - See Noradil.

Kambor - Common tongue name used by the Oracle, Golvashala, when in human form.

Kellegarn – One of the eight gods. Creator of the race of Dwarves, he loves all the earth and rocks and gems and taught his creations the ways of stone and mining.

Kerad - Powerful cleric of Loracia currently serving in the Vale of Morgoran and therefore serving Morgoran.

Kimala – Former mistress of Naneden, A spy of Enowene's spy ring.

King Amarantus - Lord and ruler of the dragons of Draegodor.

King Occelot - The somewhat sniveling, and sometimes incompetent, ruler of the kingdom of Symboria.

Kragodor - The black city. Nestled in the treacherous Mountains of Madness in Ishrak, Kragodor is home to the exiled dragons who were last known to serve Toborne.

Kyrie - Mysterious, sometimes-companion of Lady Shey. He is a Kylerie elf, which is an elf about half the size of an Arillian Elf. He loves danger and intrigue. His strange habit of showing up when events go wrong drives some people to wonder where his allegiances lie. Dorenn believes Kyrie is more than he seems.

Loracia (*LORE-race-E-uh*) - Goddess of life and mother of the gods.

Lora Daine- (lora dane) (AKA dragon stone) Stone of the dragons and dragon knights used for communication between dragons and their dragon knights over long distances. Depending on the size and magic of the stone, it can send small parties instantly across short distances. It can also sometimes be used to send its user back and forth between stones over greater distances. Dragon stones are rare to normal peasants. Only people of stature (other than the dragons and dragon knights) are allowed to use them.

Lourn – Former Innkeeper and owner of the Tiger's Head Inn in Brookhaven, Symboria. Currently the king of the Trigothian kingdom of Ardenia, Father of Dorenn Adair.

Lux Amarou - Continent in the northwest formerly inhabited by the Amar, (high men). The oldest cities of man are on Lux Amarou, but they are all mostly in ruins now and inhabited by the ghosts of the dead, among other agents of death and destruction for an age past. A few of the living still reside there, but not many.

Lux Enor - Capital of the west. Home city-state of the highlord. The highlord rules over all of Trigothia, Symboria, and what's left of Ishrak. The last highlord, Rastafin Stowe, was assassinated without leaving an heir. To avoid any power vacuums, only the magical Silver Drake can choose one worthy enough to sit on the highest throne in the land. After Rastafin Stowe, she has yet to proclaim a successor, so the throne remains vacant. A warder presides over the day-to-day affairs, but has limited power.

Malantis – One of the eight gods. Third son of Fawlsbane Vex and Loracia. God of the oceans, seas, lakes, rivers, and everything water related.

Melias - Monk of Fawlsbane Vex. Guardian and sworn protector of Dorenn Adair. Now transformed into a creature called the Brae Daun Duil.

Mindwielder/Mindwielding - Sometimes referred to as mentalism, this is what people who can use magic of the mind, with or without drawing essence, are called. One difference between a mindwielder and a wielder is that mindwielders possess the ability to talk to each other mentally (telepathy).

Morgoran- AKA Morgoran Cleareyes. Member of the holy trine (First Trine) representing man and Fawlsbane Vex. He is reputed to be the most powerful wielder who has ever lived. (Favors balance in ruling.)

Mount Aroanian - A mountain peak in the Mountains of Madness of Ishrak.

Mount Urieus - A mountain peak in the Jagged Mountains where people are sent to wait for permission from the dragons to enter into Draegodor.

Myradon - The first and most powerful gold dragon created by Fawlsbane Vex. He guards the ethereal gates of Venifyre.

Myradon Codex - The lost tome written by Myradon that contains the magic of the dragons. It contains a powerful dragon's fire spell, which is executable by potent wielders of essence.

Naneden (*Na-NEED-den*) - Symbolic leader of Scarovia. He is considered to be mad by all who know him.

Nine Cards - A simple card game enjoyed primarily in Symboria as well as parts of the Trigothian kingdoms.

Noanas - Lost race of high dwarf.

Noradil - Elven name for the shadow or jungle elves of Darovan. They migrated along with the Siladil but found the desert too open and sparse. They moved into the dense jungle of Darovan and started harvesting the plant life there to make poisons, medicines, and magical elixirs. Most apothecaries are Noradil.

Oberan (*Oh-ber-ann*) - First dragon knight of King Amarantus.

Rennon - One of Dorenn's closest friends. Apprentice to Sanmir, the apothecary of Brookhaven, Symboria. He is a powerful mind-wielder and the healer of the mindwielders formerly known as the afflicted.

Rodraq (*Rod-rack*) - Lady Shey's man-of-arms.

Rugania - Island off the coast of Sythia, across the sea from Darovan. Also called the Isle of Doom, this is the place where wielders were once trained by masters in the art of wielding. It is nicknamed the Isle of Doom because anyone trying to sneak on the isle without the wielders' consent and preparation often died before they crossed the beaches.

Sand Elves - See Siladil.

Scarovia - Kingdom east of the Jagged Mountains, home of the Scarovs, or Scarovians as some cultures call them.

Seabrey - Large port city in northern Symboria. Trade city of the north for the kingdoms of Ardenia and Sythia (see Basillain).

Seancey (*SHAWN-see*) - Ranger of Symboria stationed in the Vale of Morgoran, brother of Lady Shey.

Seandara (SHAWN-dar-a) - Princess of Endil (Foreshome). Has a reoccurring dream of Dorenn.

Shadow Elves - See Noradil.

Shadow Lurker - Pertains to a Drasmyd Duil. A nickname.

Shila - Dwarf who helped Lady Shey after she escaped her kidnappers.

Siladil - Elven name for the sand elves of Darovan. They migrated to Darovan and learned to live in the harsh desert conditions. They are notoriously hard to see while traveling across sand, and they can sink down into it as if they were submerging in water. They are fierce fighters and are almost impossible to defeat in the desert. They have darker, sun-kissed skin and light eyes. They are shorter than the Arillian elves and considered to be more primitive.

Sildariel - Stern matron, queen, and leader of the Sylvan elves of Endil.

Solicanth - The joining of two celestial beings through time. They are either a force for great good or a source for great evil. They sometimes live in harmony, but more often than not, they clash. If they live in harmony, they are usually very integral to the peace and prosperity of the kingdoms.

Steban - First dragon knight of Charna (one of King Amarantus' sisters).

Swordmaster Grint - Villager of Brookhaven who taught young village boys (and sometimes girls) the way of weapons. He was an infantry man and good friend of Lourn Adair.

Sylvalora (*SIL-va- lore-a*) - The Silver Drake, sometimes traveling companion and mentor to Lady Shey.

Symbor - Capital city of the kingdom of Symboria. This city was once called Paladine and is not to be confused with Old Symbor, which is now a ruin in the Sacred Land. Old Symbor is the original home of Shey and Seancey.

Symboria - Oldest kingdom of men on the continent proper, home to the race of men known as Are'dune, descendants of the Amar from Lux Amarou.

Tabac - The giant leaf of the tabac plant that is shredded, dried, and cured to fill a pipe.

Tatrice – Former kitchen maiden in the Tiger's Head Inn in Brookhaven, Symboria. Currently she is the first female dragon knight and the first dragon knight of Shadesilver the white dragon.

Toborne - Member of the holy trine (First Trine) representing Aedreagnon and the Scarovs. He tried to steal the Silver Drake but failed. (Favors cut-throat politics and ruling by fear.)

Trendan - Half-elven friend of Dorenn from the realm of the woodland elves. He has lived in Brookhaven most of his life.

Theosus Fiderea - A dragon hidden in Trigothia as an apothecary.

The Archers of Endil - Elven archers from the city of Endil (Foreshome) who have built a reputation as the most feared archers ever known. They are of the Eridil (Sylvan elves) and have never known defeat.

The Defenders - Similar to the Enforcers except that they only patrol the Sacred Land.

The Enforcers - A band of men dedicated to enforcing the law against magic in Symboria and Trigoth the city. The Enforcers are dwindling in numbers and are not actively recruiting. They are considered abominations by those who are left that can wield essence because they are also essence wielders who chose to follow a very different path, which is unforgivable.

The Great Sythian Forest - Huge forest stretching the whole length of the coast of Sythia from north to south. It is the home of the Eridil, among other creatures.

The Isle of Doom - See Rugania.

The Jagged Mountains - Huge mountain range that separates Scarovia and Abaddonia from the West. It is the home of dwarves, Dramyds, and Drasmyd Duil, among others.

The Lost Army - The army of the North and West, lost near a city called Anisport, a whole continent away from where they should be.

The Mountains of Madness - Mountain range in the northern part of Ishrak. Not only are these mountains infested with orcs and foul beasts but it is also home to the black city of Kragodor, city of the fallen (evil) dragons.

The Sacred Land - Huge tract of land once belonging to Symboria that hosted the War of the Oracle and was devastated into a wasteland unable to support life or feed essence for wielders. It is guarded as a reminder of what magic can do to the land and is the reason magic use was outlawed in the southern kingdoms.

The Sea Goddess - A wooden clipper ship captained by Felladane and first officer Edifor.

The Silver Drake - A statuette made of pure silver inset with ruby eyes made by the First Trine to select the one man worthy of leading the kingdoms of the West as overlord or highlord. The gods themselves took up the Silver Drake and each bestowed into it their own gift. It is unknown what many of the gods' gifts were, but the goddess of life, Loracia, gave the Silver Drake the gift of life. Fawlsbane Vex gave it a will and mind of its own.

Tolennor Forest - Forest southwest of the Vale of Morgoran. It is haunted and cursed. The cursed village of Signal Hill was located in this forest.

Tome of Enlightenment - Tome given to man by the god Fawls-bane Vex, laying down the guidelines and ability for man to do magic.

Trigoth - Once the capital city of Trigothia, it was split into three sectors each belonging to the three Trigothian kingdoms of Adracoria, Ardenia, and Sythia.

Trigothia - Ancient kingdom of the three major houses of Are'dune men. In the civil wars, the three families separated the kingdom into the three kingdoms of Ardenia (Arden family), Sythia (Arasyth family), and Adracoria (Adrac family).

Trine – *Definition* - A group of three. The First Trine is the three first disciples: Morgoran, Ianthill, and Toborne.

Tyre - City near Seabrey, Symboria. Last city before advancing to Mount Urieus.

Vale of Morgoran - Vale with the Tower of Morgoran at its center. Once the tower stood there alone, but after Morgoran was cursed to see only the future, a small village cropped up at the tower's base and expanded. People hoped that Morgoran could cure their loved ones or predict their future. Even though Morgoran is no longer cursed, the village still functions and remains.

Venifyre (*Ven-nee-fear*) - Realm and home of the gods. In ancient dragon-speak first created by the gods, *y* is represented as an *ea* sound, so Venifyre is not pronounced *Ven-nee-fire* but *Ven-nee-fear*. So Genidyre would be pronounced *Jin-nee-dear*, not *Jin-nee-dire*.

Veric Namear - An assassin and father of Lady Shey. He was forced against his will to abandon his family when Sheyna was still a toddler.

Vesperin - Orphaned cleric of Loracia from Brookhaven, Symboria, and close friend of Dorenn.

Vetell Fex - Monastery located in Symboria, named after the brother of the god Vex. Vetell Fex simply means Fex's home.

War of the Oracle - A war started by Golvashala (the Oracle) to rid the land of magic so he could take over and rule. He was defeated and presumed dead. (This war created The Sacred Land.)

Winterhaven - A festive winter holiday in the Trigothian kingdoms Symboria, Ishrak, Darovan, and Arillia. It is a popular date to get married in the Trigothian kingdoms.

Wielding - The ability to magically draw essence from everything around that contains essence and wield it to accomplish higher functioning magical feats. Drawing too much essence from one area may devoid that area of its ability to replenish essence for a longer period of time. Unless one is a mindwielder, areas devoid of essence are therefore devoid of magic. Areas of devastation come back with greater amounts of essence.

Xeian – One of the eight gods. The middle son and co-creator of the race of elves, lover of trees and green and things that grow.

Printed in June 2023
by Rotomail Italia S.p.A., Vignate (MI) - Italy